Dream Catcher

Dream Catcher

Patricia Legaré Hare

Northwest Publishing, Inc.
Salt Lake City, Utah

Dream Catcher

All rights reserved.
Copyright © 1996 Northwest Publishing, Inc.

Reproduction in any manner, in whole or in part,
in English or in other languages, or otherwise
without written permission of the publisher is prohibited.

This is a work of fiction.
All characters and events portrayed in this book are fictional,
and any resemblance to real people or incidents is purely coincidental.

For information address: Northwest Publishing, Inc.
6906 South 300 West, Salt Lake City, Utah 84047

J. B. 3-10-95
C. R.

PRINTING HISTORY
First Printing 1996

ISBN: 1-56901-554-6

NPI books are published by Northwest Publishing, Incorporated,
6906 South 300 West, Salt Lake City, Utah 84047.
The name "NPI" and the "NPI" logo are trademarks belonging to
Northwest Publishing, Incorporated.

PRINTED IN THE UNITED STATES OF AMERICA.
10 9 8 7 6 5 4 3 2 1

*"When we sleep, good and bad dreams float over us.
The dream catcher is hung by the sleeping area
where it catches your dreams in a web.
Bad dreams are held in the web
until morning while good
dreams come to you
down the feather."*

—Ojibway grandmother

One

Down the beach in the ruddy glow of the setting sun two children squealed and dodged February's cold waves. I picked up a stick, tossed it as far as I could and turned my back to the roaring ocean, remembering two other children who would never laugh and play again. Delilah loped after her prize, her big feet kicking up sprays of sand, her pink tongue flapping from her open mouth. Would the painful memories ever leave? Never totally, the psychiatrist warned. "And for decency's sake, they shouldn't!" I'd argued, but he urged me not to waste too much time seeking forgiveness for the suffering I'd caused.

The big, oafish dog grabbed the driftwood and wheeled,

bringing it to me. "Good girl," I said, patting her head. She sprinted out. I hurled the stick again and ambled along the water's edge watching my jerky shadow stretch far ahead. Physically, I'm almost normal compared to six months ago, when I hobbled stiffly with a cane. Patching up my broken, long-neglected right leg only lowered me a smidgen under my original five-eleven, I've added back all but ten pounds of my original one seventy-five, and I'm alive; even survived six nightmarish years in a prisoner-of-war camp. The North Koreans would have found me no matter what. If only I'd stayed in that damned jungle, a whole family might be alive today, too.

A movement up at my house broke into my black preoccupation. I looked up. There, Rhea leaned over the deck's rail, her face hidden by the wide brim of her familiar straw hat, and she waved a tan, lean arm back and forth. Never dreaming I would miss her like I had, my heart speeded up like I'd just raced with the children down the shore, and I wanted to run to her. Instead, I raised my arm, returned her greeting and headed in her direction. Watching her bound down the steps, fear clawed at my insides. Not like in the camp fearing for my life, more like a forest bird freed in a treeless desert, running out of reserve. What if her agent, Lowell, of the Philadelphia Armbrester's—which he so concisely throws into every introduction—pushed her to set their wedding date? After all, they announced their engagement over a year ago, and if I were Lowell I would be tying her down.

Everything must be all right though. In an earthbound cloud of white garments her sleek body sways from side to side with each quick step, rushing toward me!

The day's blazing fireball disappeared, shadows darkened her bare arms, calves and feet—already island native bronze—and I knew time and distance would never whet my appetite, prayed the swiftness in her gait said the same. She's getting close, and I need to decide what I am going to say—and do.

My older sister, Charlotte, didn't make any bones about not liking Rhea and scoffed when I complained about her prolonged business trip, but Charlotte's changed. Even on that first hospital visit her crisp welcome bordered on annoyance. Her dark, almond shaped eyes—that she and I acquired from Mom's Cherokee ancestry—darted all around the room except at me, and when she did glance my way, they were muddy with what I'd chalked up to emotion—anger the furthest cause from my mind. At least my kid sister, Natalie, is fond of Rhea, although at first she experienced some suspicions. While I lolled in the hospital, Nat, complying with my wishes, rented and fixed up my seaside abode, turned around one day to find Rhea standing in the doorway, offering a conch shell along with her name. Enthralled, Nat described her as dark,—possibly Polynesian—a full, copper-colored mouth, Siberian cold blue eyes and scrawny. Her last adjective was so typical of Nat! Because we're a large-boned, square-faced family with coarse hair ranging from Mom's brown-black to Dad's blond British tendencies, Nat thinks everyone else is malnourished. Also typical—Nat's inherent need to make singles into couples—she'd invited Rhea to dinner, who, to hear Natalie's story, declined rather brusquely. But Randy, the youngest of our foursome, thinks Rhea is neat, but says our livelihood will stay more solid if I'm uninvolved. Sometimes I think Randy's eye for business is founded on greed and marginally criminal. I need to make him understand I'm a deck hand on his charter fishing boat; nothing more or less.

A blast of evening wind ripped Rhea's hat away but she paid no attention. The moment the sun vanished, the temperature dropped, nipped my hands, and the sand-chilled Arctic Ocean cold beneath my bare feet. But seeing her, my blood boiled like Vesuvius' lava.

I'll let her make the first move, I thought, but wanted to whoop aloud when she sprang into my arms. I whirled her around. When I released her, I lived dangerously for a second and leaned toward her mouth. She tensed and offered her cheek. Careful! You'll screw up! I kissed her forehead lightly and whispered, "Damn, I've missed you!"

Smoothly but stealthily, she pushed away. Again, ominous fear constricted my already dry throat. What if Lowell convinced her she would sell more paintings living in Philadelphia or New York—or worse—abroad? Hoping to keep her mind off my nemesis or whatever crushing news I expected her to confess, I meant to divert her. Instead, I blurted, "How was Philly?"

She wedged her shoulder under my arm, lightly placed one arm around my waist, and got in step with me. Welcoming her warmth, I set my imagination loose. My skin tingled where hers touched. I treasured sensations ranging from wild to soft and breathed in her gingery scent.

"Oh, Mike, I hated it, and its snobs!"

For the time being this would do, but deep down I knew someday her money-wielding patrons would dangle one too many gold-plated carrots—namely fame—before her eyes, and she would go. But now, holding her away, I smiled bravely and challenged, "Aww, come on!"

"All I could think about was running barefoot on our beach with its natural law and order, its strengths, its surprises. Lowell's furious with me! Called me an 'incorrigible lapwing shrew.'"

Good shot, Lowell, old buddy! Our future's looking brighter! She locked her arm in mine and we started toward the house.

"I looked it up. It's some Old World bird related to the plover family. Of course, I knew a shrew's an obstinate woman, so I called him and said, 'Thank you, but I have one question. Am I a summer or winter lapwing?'" Clapping her hand over her mouth, she giggled. "I knew I had him. He didn't know what to say, so I pounded torment deeper into his flimsy case. 'Summer is white-bellied. Winter is black. Which one am I?' He answered, 'You're just incorrigible. Call me when you're sane.' And I replied, 'That may be never!'"

Watching her play games with her elongated shadow, I admitted to myself she did have some birdlike qualities: her brown hair coiled in a nestlike crown with corkscrewed wisps escaping here and there; her shadowy raven's eyes examining every flurry within range; and her primal habitat with hulking leafy plants—where I suspected she sheltered bat-winged Pterodactyls. In this, implant all-consuming maroon chairs and diffused lighting, her pottery collection, bowls of fruit, folds of beige and olive green framing her windows, and she has fashioned her own private forest. The exception: her stark studio, desolate of color. But I would cut out my tongue before I would agree with Lowell.

She lured me along, her head bobbing from side to side, scooped up her hat, and slapped it on her head. "Aren't you proud of me?"

"Yes," I vowed, wanting her not to talk about Lowell or act like somebody's twittery and superficial sister. "And I'm glad you're back."

"Is that all? Just glad I'm back?"

"No." This is your chance. Stop, pull her to you, tell her, before this nonsense goes any further. But I didn't. "I'm beside myself with joy. Did you sell your paintings?"

"Almost every one! I think they are shipping back two."

"This deserves a celebration." You coward! Do you think she can read your mind? "How about dinner at The Summerhouse?"

"Nooo. Too stuffy. How about Sloopy's?"

From the jukebox, Johnny Ray wailed, "When your sweetheart sends a letter of good-bye…" and I reached over to wipe ketchup off her chin. Mid-air she grabbed my hand and growled, "How many women have you softened up with these juicy hamburgers full of odorous onions while I slaved away in the North?"

A transition from prey to predator; a feline flexing her claws. "Hundreds," I answered tersely, getting somewhat annoyed with her attitude.

"I knew it!" She looked away, watched the broad waitress with white broom-sage hair twist between the tables, her crepe soled shoes squeaking on the black and white checked linoleum. "Have you slept with her?" The woman heard. Scowling over her shoulder first at me, then Rhea, half her age, she smiled, flaunting a gold rimmed tooth.

I shrank into the chrome and red plastic chair and muttered, "No. Do you want me to?"

"Stick to Nurse Tess…"

"Rhea!"

"Was it Tess' idea that you cut your hair?"

Sighing, I realized she would never forget the birthday party incident, or let me. Of course that unforgettable day, I nearly croaked when I discovered Tess had answered the door in my robe and invited Rhea and my sisters in. Spying the presumed cake in the traditional square white box Natalie held by a string, a shameless Tess offered to make coffee. The girls declined, but making matters worse, Tess peeked into the bathroom where I—unsuspecting—showered. My first clue to the shockwave rumbling below the surface in the other room came when I heard Tess call out, Hey, girls, wait! He's up and coming! Who would blame them for leaving the scene? Birthdays can be a bitch even when you're not in prison. "No, my idea. Warmer weather headed our way and all. Would you like another beer?"

"No. Take me home. I'm drunk on good, honest people like the homely waitress, Jimmy in the kitchen who makes these ptomaine-burgers, red tides and blue moons. I wanna light a fire, sip white wine and listen to you tell me what you've been doing for the last one hundred years."

Inside my truck, a long, uneasy silence drew up my shoulders like a tightly twisted rubber band. And like our conversation all evening long, the headlights bounced erratically on the waterfront road. For a moment I believed she'd fallen asleep, and stole glimpses. Eyes closed, her head doddered against the window, her body palsied by worn out shocks and the concrete road eroded by wind, salt and use. Overhead, a cloud umbrella of moisture and ice particles blocked out the westward drifting galaxies. Gas, dust, and light-years diminished into a milky haze, and I wished we were alone on the dim planet until she blurted, "Mike, when are you going to tell me about your marriage and the POW camp?"

Why tonight? In the past, I'd managed to side-step her quizzes, but swallowing any hope for reprieve, I wisecracked, "Never," expecting her eyes to pop open.

They did. She bolted upright, punched my biceps hard and slumped back, her lower lip protruding. "I'll never let you watch me paint again either."

"You make me sit across the room now, tell me to 'Shut up' when you don't like what I say, and eat in front of me. I'll be better off."

"You're jealous!"

"Of what, your apple and spoonful of peanut butter lunches? Give me a break!"

"Remember the night of my Christmas party when you saved my social worth by unstopping my sink?" I nodded. "If you recall, that's when you not only let it slip, you proved your fixing-up skills."

Knowing she would reward me with quirky insight, I almost didn't mind her spontaneity. Who knows, I might even feel better afterwards—or more bewildered than before—like the day I cross-examined her about why she wanted to marry Lowell. Time and again I heard her openly mock him, calling him her "agent and/or fiancée" and when I asked, she replied, The better to control her career. Then I asked if she loved him. Baffling me further, she'd looked me in the eye and said she couldn't allow that to be a prerequisite, following up with, Do you understand? I said yes, but I didn't. The scheme rang alien to her usual clear-headed logic, so I probed with When? When she responded, Hopefully not for a long time, I wanted to shout, How can you be so stupid?! But now, she waited patiently for my answer and I grumbled, "Let what slip?"

She twisted on the seat, and I felt war in the air. "Where are you tonight? You said you and your wife bought a fifty year old house and something always needed fixing, and that's when you learned to."

"My place or yours?" I switched off the ignition and waited.

"Do you have white wine?"

"And firewood."

While I stoked my rendition of Hades, she quizzed me about the sticks, string, and butcher's paper strewn over my living room. "Runaway sails," I answered, thankful for the chance to get her mind on a new subject. Eagerness lit her face, and I told her about Charlotte's children wanting a kite, and so I'd spent one rainy Saturday at the library researching their construction. "That's how it all came about—fishing boats losing their sails. The problem is, now seven other kids' parents have called for kites, too. I told them I would on one condition: the kids must help. So while we work, I tell them a few tales I dug up at the library." She begged for a example, and I began. "Well, back around 1000 B. C., the Chinese engineered a wooden bird that flew for three days without falling. Several hundred years later, kites equipped with noise makers—probably made out of bamboo strips—were set loose one night and frightened off a warring adversary."

She refilled our wine glasses, returned, and squatted facing me, her full skirt spilling between her knees. "And…"

"Well, let's see. Once there was a Japanese thief who flew in a kite. He stole golden scales from an ornamental dolphin on the Emperor's castle. When the soldiers captured him, he and his whole family were boiled in oil."

"My God! You didn't tell those children that, did you?"

"Sure. They need to know stealing is wrong."

"So your parables are supposed to keep them in line?" I nodded. "Go on."

"Another story says a samurai warrior, exiled with his son, helped the boy escape on a kite. And Korean parents believe that if they write the name and birth date of each male child on paper kites and let them go, bad luck and evil spirits sail away, too. What's more, they believed that if someone found the kite and picked it up, the new owner inherited the former's maladies."

Then she picked up bits and pieces, asking what they were. I showed her how I checked the spars' symmetry by balancing the stick on a knife edge. While she fingered the brightly colored tassels I'd made for the points, I showed her how I marked the center and sandpapered away discrepancies. Next, I rubbed the kite's cover-paper against itself, explaining how it would make the substance more pliable, and she acknowledged its softness when she smoothed it out.

Later, lulled by the fire's warmth and the easy-bodied Sauvignon Blanc I keep on hand especially for her, we gazed into the iridescent flames. Taking advantage of the quiet, I drifted back to the evening she mentioned earlier, positive the incident would come up again.

On that particular twilight, I'd just started working for Randy. Still tiring easily, I'd come home, added a few boards to Delilah's new house, eaten and fallen asleep in my hammock after appreciating a fairy tale sunset. When the telephone rang, I jumped. Inside, I snatched up the receiver, and on the other end, sounding panicky, Rhea babbled about guests coming in less than an hour and her flooded kitchen. To myself, I denied grogginess from too little sleep. To her, pleased she'd called me for whatever reason, I promised rescue. I dressed and trudged across the dune between our houses lugging my tool box and a plunger.

I fixed the pipe, planning to slip out the back when I finished, but before I could she entered and asked the loaded question, Where had I learned to do all those handyman things? Without thinking I'd recalled the old house Mandy and I once owned. Rhea had tilted her head to one side and eyed me suspiciously. "I thought you weren't married." She was remembering our first meeting when I'd volunteered that information, but I figured surely by now Natalie must have filled her in on all the gory details so I replied breezily, "Not now. Was once." Narrowed, beady eyes raced across my face, but then her kooky friend, Rebecca, burst through the kitchen door, saving the day.

"Are you in pain?"
"No. Why?"
"You seem uncomfortable."
"Sorry. I'm a lousy host tonight."
"It's called stalling. Anyway, it's time we got back to the original subject. All I know is you're thirty-seven years old, you were once married, you spent nearly six years in a Korean POW camp, you're a deck hand on your younger brother's charter boat, and that's all you ever intend to do. And, oh, yes. You have this bead and feather, twig and

twine doohickey above your bed; a token I understand some good-hearted Ojibway grandmother created to filter out bad dreams."

I laughed. "Which you donated."

"Trying to win your trust."

Two

He had been saved again, but if I had to wait around until spring I would pull the story out of this mulish man.

While he and Natalie talked, I answered when necessary but mostly nosed around the room, half-heartedly listening to their conversation. I picked up the tarnished picture frame I'd studied many times. In it, Mike's chocolate-hued hair, now long and wavy, barely showed below the stiff Air Force cap. Natalie told me that when he was little their parents kept it in a crew cut and that they, his siblings, never realized it was curly until after he'd been declared Missing In Action. Then, with their parents, they spent hours reminiscing through photo albums, and seeing the tike with chestnut ringlets, doubted any correlation to the Mike they knew. Testimony to this fact, his mother, or perhaps Mandy, had placed one brown curl tied with a blue ribbon in this frame.

Natalie revealed a great deal about Mike that day, but little affecting the two questions I wanted him to answer tonight. Her intent—eagerly nudging Mike and me together, the sooner the better—aroused my curiosity, and I felt sure she exaggerated for my benefit saying her memories of him were the "brawny but tender, meek but strong-willed, patient but visionary, older brother." Whatever, I wasn't sure whether she was indeed a matchmaker or sincerely believed we were a predestined duo.

No longer than I've known Mike, anger is the only kink I've uncovered in his near flawless personality, and knowing bits and pieces of the circumstances under which he survived, who could blame him for that! Certainly not I. It's hard enough for me to understand why that dimpled-cheeked, strong-jawed man in the snapshot, the same moving toward me now, had had to bear such hardships as the Air Force revealed to his family. Surely they searched for their men? Were the jungles so impregnable it took them that long to find him? Couldn't the U.S. have demanded proof that their servicemen weren't being held prisoners?

We may have tried our hand defending against Communist aggression in that combative land, but evidently the Chinese military, coupled with the Soviet Union's support, were more than we could out-maneuver. For once, our reputedly superior nation plainly met its match. The funny thing was, every time I tried to blame Mike's long imprisonment on weak politics or defective military strategy, his unfaltering loyalty stupefied me, even when I'd quote statistics like: Korea, the burial ground for 20,000 Americans, probably many more; America's asinine outrage upon learning her troops crumbled under psychological brainwashing;

and that although the Armistice's voluntary prisoner repatriation point had been accepted, it failed to unify North and South Korea, bring about the withdrawal of foreign troops, or flush out allied hordes being held captive. Still, after all this, not to mention the atrocities cited over and over by the media, Mike remained faithful.

But survive he did, and some vague words of Emerson's to do with the Past not sleeping, about rays of light shooting up from long-buried years, caused me to glance his way.

"Rhea?"

I set the portrait down, took the wine glass he held out and said, "Thanks." Comfort for a ravished soul; loosing blanketed hatred—Was that what I sought for him? That, and erasing that maddening vacancy in his eyes whenever I brought up his imprisonment. No medicine, no elixirs, no witch doctors, just the two of us pulling out all stops; exorcising his nightmares.

Although there's no sign now of closeted pain, I know denial, an offshoot of his anger, can wear concealment's mask as easily as the revealing one. A fine shaman he would make for others, unable to confront his own dragons! Right up there with Carl Jung, the Greeks' Plato and Socrates, he could match each in teachings when it came to what is happy is sad, what is sad is happy; a Tragedy and Comedy natural. But his role is not an act, although I do think he is ill-suited to deal with the hurt he'd have everyone believe he so cleverly conceals.

Over the last seven months I've witnessed some of the real scars, and like the deceptive tip of the iceberg, I know the more painful misery lurks just below the surface.

Tonight, before Natalie arrived, I asked him if the threatening letters and voodoolike plunderings were still happening. When he said yes, I shivered, and once again feared for his person, confused by the spiteful acts.

On a more humorous side, Mike hounds me for stories of

the "beat generation," making me go into great detail describing their trash pile clothes, their "pads," their slang, their self-proclaimed mysticism, and their raccoon-eyed girls. He'll smile, and the two deepest scars on his face totally disappear in laugh lines, and slowly, from deep in his tummy he chuckles and I just know he's going to let out a Santa's Ho, Ho, Ho! and for a few moments life is a little less serious. But then it's gone, and he's uneasy. I spout more trivia he missed out on like "squares are out, a square is someone who smokes without taking the band off his cigar" or "wears a pocket handkerchief with his initials showing" and is the opposite of someone "far out," just to see him smile, much less laugh again.

But tonight, robust, full of life and tan, he turns to Natalie, hands her a glass of milk and a plate with a man-sized sandwich, and they exchange a special, soundless grin. He's fooled her, because she really believes he's cured! Standing here in the background, I see their unique camaraderie, but Mike's words about Natalie and Max stumbling into a gold mine with their restaurant business, volunteering the information that both possess limited financial expertise, haunts me, just like the war that ended where it began, haunts Mike. In spite of modest fame among locals, their out-of-the-way Gautier's Bay Restaurant doesn't exactly lure tourists, and I question what has spawned their apparent prosperity.

Sighing, I dropped into one of Mike's pair of butterfly chairs—magenta covering black wrought iron—and look around. Very little in this room reflects Mike's taste. Knowing Natalie outfitted his Shangri-La, I see it matches her persona right down to her lipstick and nail polish. He thinks she's wonderful, but I can tell his sister hasn't the remotest idea that Mike suffers through holistic sounding threats, hellish nightmares and periodic melancholy. Maybe disclosing these aggravations to me eases his mind but you would think his family could sense some of his distress.

Still, I'd prefer to see Mike's passion winging around this room; his choice of colors, his choice of style. On the other hand, maybe like most men, he is comfortable in whatever ambiance is chosen for him.

Eyeing the kindred and their tête-à-tête discreetly, to myself I admit resenting this intrusion. Earlier, when Natalie beeped her horn, he had gone out and waved her in. She sprang up the steps, situated her tall, pale—yet hearty—self in a green canvas chair—which does look more like Mike's choice—and announced her backbone was rubbing her ribs. I actually snorted, but no one noticed.

Now, upbraiding her, Mike asked, "What are you doing out so late and by yourself?"

Natalie purred and petted him like her latest creation, making her appear adoring. Then she launched into another of her bratty colloquies: she and her friends just saw the most boring movie, but her alternative would have been listening to Max and his accountant dredge through restaurant paperwork, so, she thought she'd see what her darling brother was up to!

I had joined her "darling" in the kitchen, and together we rummaged the refrigerator to prepare his "guest's" meal, all the while knowing Mike would die if he knew I was such a bigot. Wearing our own Machiavellian mask tonight, aren't we? To keep from gagging, I concentrated on the knotted muscles in his forearms when he lifted a large ham and set it on the counter. Now he's handing me cheese and apples and I laughed to myself, thinking how he ridicules my meals.

I tried to imagine the Mike I know with a full beard, hair to his shoulders and skeletally thin while passively listening to their dialogue: discussing the cafe's new garbage disposal; Boeing's 707 airliner flying nonstop from New York to London; and finally, James Dean's worldwide-mourned death. While Mike fixed her sandwich, I washed her apple and noticed he radiated good health. "...and over the years," Natalie vowed months back, "when Charlotte and Randy scolded when I'd talk about him like he was alive, I never doubted he wasn't. Even the dark pits surrounding his sparkling eyes couldn't hide the truth from us though." At that point she'd reminisced about his tears of relief upon seeing his family. Then, learning the awful news about Mandy, at which time she gave me a sketchy story about the divorce and Mandy remarrying—they feared he'd gone insane. Sedated, he had seemed reconciled, and even when he came home from the hospital and with the passage of time, she declared he'd never brought the subject up again, so neither had they. I found her comments unnervingly nonchalant, however, this all helped me understand my feelings toward her, but I longed to hear Mike's version.

As of tonight, seeing these two interact, I realized this fragile-featured, outspoken blonde and this gentle, tawny-skinned man whose face bears the abruptness of an American Indian, shared something deeper than devotion. First of all, I reminded myself, Blood's thicker than water! But there's something more. Could it be she's jealous? I suppose that's possible. Of me? Hardly. Apart, they seem at opposite poles, and certainly she and I vie for his attention for wholly different reasons, but then again, I wouldn't put jealousy past her for selfishness sake if nothing else. And whether or not Natalie covers up some cloaked fear, or she really is superficial, I know better than to confront this Waterloo, Mike's adored baby sister.

Mike slid the glass door open, picked up the tray of cheese and crackers I'd prepared and motioned us to come outside. A crisp wind whistled into the room. Natalie and I grimaced and chattered, "Brrrr" in unison.

"You weaklings!" he teased, and I noticed a drop of sweat running from his hairline, around the curve of his square jaw and down his neck. "Jeez, can I at least leave the door open? This blaze is driving me out."

Natalie, with her mouth full, mumbled and nodded. My time to nurture, I suggested he take off his sweater. "Wonder why I didn't think of that?" he replied, yanking it over his head. Again I noticed his hair no longer brushed his shirt collar, and I made a mental note to tell him I liked it long!

Now he's telling Natalie about my latest painting. I can tell he's proud, says the little boy and girl look just like Sonny and Shallie, Charlotte's children, but adds he still isn't sure who the other person is. Obstinate man! But he had been truly shocked when I said, "You!" So while fragments of their conversation, "...captured the Coppertone ad quality of Sonny's skin. ...Shallie's sun-washed hair and pale eyes..." drifts to me, I want to shout, I don't care what you think, you're in it! And, boy, if you doubt that, are you in for a surprise at my next exhibit!

While they exchange pseudo-commentaries, I recalled a rare moment when Natalie and I actually communed. One warm November day last year, she and I waded through the surf coming in from skin diving, and she said, "Look at him, Rhea. He's in love with you." Mike stood at the water's edge holding towels. I remembered him telling her not to forget them, and already thinking myself catty for vaguely disliking this cunning Amazon, I decided she'd probably forgotten them intentionally. But more than a little curious about her remark, I chose to study Mike's face. "Think so, huh?"

"I know it. And don't deny it, you love him."

"Hmmm," I replied flippantly, feeling like a teenager.

When we reached him, I said, "You look hot," threw my wet hair over and shook my head like a dog. Beads of water flew his way. "How about a dip?"

He laughed good-naturedly. "Just got one, thanks." Remembering the day like it just happened, I can still see crystalline drops hanging from his nose, chin and the tips of his hair, and I wondered how anyone could threaten this man. "I've got supper ready, and here are a pair of big-time hungries," he said, tousling the hair of the two blond headed tots bouncing beside him. Intrigued by his love for his older sister's children, but weighing my growing paranoia regarding his family, I contemplated their mother's attitude, too. At Mike's insistence, I'd joined their company several times in the past, and given Charlotte's insensitive gruffness, it seemed to me she and Julian abused Mike's willingness to baby-sit more and more. On the other hand, Mike seemed oblivious to this, and I'd reminded myself again: This is a family affair, and none of my business!

On my own, I'd unearthed the knowledge that Mike had been to his grandparents what Thomas Edison was to electricity. Sadly, they both died during his absence, but I'd listened to his sweet reminiscing and wondered if giving him up for dead, did they drop all their worldly goods into Charlotte, Natalie and Randy's laps? Was he too easy-going to think this might be cause for Charlotte's exasperating hostility, Natalie's showy adoration and Randy's ludicrous gift of a job on his precious charter boat? Did it never enter their trout-sized brains that Mike deserved at least some small, personal keepsake of those two he had so steadfastly worshipped? In spite of any feeling he might have about my theories,—should I dare express them—I knew him well enough to know he would never dream of asking for a fair share, and considering my own cheerless background, I labeled his brother and sisters first-rate phonies.

Meanwhile, engrossed in my suspicions that day on the beach, I had fallen behind while Sonny and Shallie skipped around him. Many times since that day, I'd poured over this, and once, Mike and I even discussed the occasion, startling me with his rendition. He didn't remember the towel incident, only the little boy holding up his bucket, showing Mike his prized find, and Mike innocently suggesting they use his fiddler crabs in the gumbo he planned for the next day. Mike recalled Sonny freezing, his faded eyes darkening, and the half-hidden sun shimmering golden in a quick tear.

I did remember Mike stopping, walking back and dropping to his knees before the child. He'd taken Sonny's thin shoulders in his hands, looked at the boy and said, "Hey, you want to keep them for pets?" The small head bobbed. "Then I've got just the thing. There's a big glass bowl in the pantry, big enough for them all. We'll add some sand and put in a jar top or something for water. We'll make them an island paradise." A balled-up fist wiped the tear. Mike stood up and rubbed the boy's back between his shoulder blades. Taking Sonny's hand and offering Shallie his other, the three walked ahead, talking softly. Natalie and I followed. Suddenly, Mike jumped out ahead of them, duck-walking backwards. I wondered what he was telling them when he straightened out his arms like airplane wings, rolled them up, down and around. The children cackled. Sonny mimicked Mike's aerobatics, and all three laughed.

The reason I remembered that part was because he'd done that to me, too—not the antics—just facing me, walking backwards. Then he argued. "You can't mean that! 'Joshua's Law' is great. More blue might throw it off balance—don't you think?" he added cautiously.

I'd stifled my impulse to declare, "You've never had an art lesson in your life!" and said, "I'm sure if I just put a dab more..." But later that same night, after deliberately inviting him to dinner, I'd taken my palette knife and added blue. The painting grew cold and one-sided. Reluctantly, I applied a streak or two of green. "Joshua's Law" still struggled in coolness, but some of the weight left. Mike whispered, "More." I glared at him, but I did it. He moved to the opposite wall, leaned against the bookcase and murmured, "Come here and look." I moved to his side. He put his hand on my shoulder, and I saw he was right. These were my jumbled recollections: emotions ranging from resentment to tenderness.

Suddenly, I realized Natalie had asked me about the children's portrait. Mike stared at me as if I spoke a foreign language when I told her I was having trouble with their skin; that it's difficult to capture. He jumped up and began pacing. "She's too modest, Nat. I don't know what it's going to take to make her quit ridiculing herself and her work." Facing his sister, and as if I wasn't in the room, he asked, "Is that some insecurity peculiar to artists or just a ploy to get compliments?"

Natalie shrugged. "Ask her!"

After I told his sister good-bye, I watched them walk side by side to her car. He strides with the youthfulness of a boy. Natalie skipped to keep up, barked at him and he slowed. They talked for a while in the glow of a big white moon and I thought of the day I'd first seen him with Tess, the nurse. Of course I didn't know who she was then; I learned that when she introduced herself on his birthday! Restless myself that twilight long ago, I'd spied him roaming the dunes like a Nomad, chin high, the sky his audience. He squatted, reached out and scooped up a handful of burnt sand. He squeezed the damp grains, then opened his outstretched hand and let the wind rip them to Merlin's Tomb on the cliffs of Cornwall, or wherever his mind wandered.

By then the stage was set and my eyes were prisoners. Like a neurosurgeon examining a famous brain, I wondered what patterns he saw in the water, sand and sky; what tenor the ocean's music played to his ears and for what his soul yearned. Buffeted by the wind, he rose and walked toward the surf. Did sirens' voices tempt him to their distant shores? Or maybe Poe's "City in the Sea" lured him to its watery arms, offering to caress him with exotic oils and slippery grasses. Quite carried away, I noticed the wind finger his wood thrush's brown hair, and I wanted to go to him. Although he's told me nothing, I know he's locked those wasted years away in a solitary chamber and I longed to help him forget. Suddenly fearful, I headed for the door, intending to rush out and save him from seeking the depths sandy bottom, cheat Neptune of his last breath and tell him... What?

That's when the prima donna appeared. Standing on the crest of a dune, the wind blew her brassy hair, fluttered her skimpy apparel, and she bounded down the powdery sand. Then I knew jealousy! I prayed for Satan's army to grab her ankles and drag her to the waiting furnaces jaws! Or maybe if I just twitched my nose... Instead, she sneaked up to where he stooped, unnoticed until she slipped her arms over his shoulders. Surprised, he rose, and when he turned, a dainty foot, followed by a slender leg, lifted and wrapped around his body like a carnival snake. One arm slithered to his hair, the other around his waist, and at the same time—as though she were trying via assimilation to become part of him—all over him. He steadied her, pulled her close, blotting out the splinters of light between them. She's no stranger, that's for sure! I closed my eyes, but opened them again quickly. My heart raced inside my body while I pretended it was my lips he chose, my thigh he held and pressed against his hard body.

You are jealous, Rhea! No, I have no claim on him! Do you think she just materialized? Conceivable. But truth's sour juices surged up my throat.

White wings flashed. Mistaking them for anger, I watched three gulls glide by and listened to their screams. Inside, and alone, my finger outlined the memory of his face on the windowpane, and that Jezebel broke away and ran. Confused, he brushed a hand over his forehead, and following her lead, disappeared between the dunes. She'll win. He'll win. I'll lose.

Darkness sponged away rosy shadows, and I quickly switched on the light, obliterating the scene on the beach, but not before I went a little insane. Get back to work, you busybody! But what I wanted was to kneel and pull him down in the warm sand with me, whispering words he would think he had dreamed—Study your sketch, you fool!—and spread over him with velvety caresses while the waves sang.

The night grew quiet, and amazed by my erotic craving, I worked frantically on the fog curling through my crone's swampy forest. Blessed be the darkness! My brush skipped to the silvery trails of freeloading Spanish moss. Quick! Mix equal parts of red, blue, and yellow. Load a clean brush with the new black for the tree-lined swamp and…Save yourself the anguish!…swat at the tumbledown, empty house he said—Damn!—made him want to fix its rotting neglect. Queer emotion, anger. Inside, everything's turning muddy! Outside, even the breakers seem easy, but my imagination built on what I knew was happening beneath the cobalt sky while I slapped a thick coat of envy on my canvas. My painting evolved, not sunny and buoyant like the love I'd planned; not quite as bleak as hate, but just as detrimental, and coupled with its sister, spite, I sensed how easily a world could fall apart and finished my gloomy portrayal.

That night I couldn't help but ponder my own destiny. Serenity lost, I picked up my brush, wiped its bristles with my flecked cloth, remembering how he called those blues and purples "wizardry." My hands trembled. My intellect shouted, It's none of your business! Forlornly, my rendering sat on the high ground of reality, back from the reed-lined river of desire, feeding and sucking up the bayous of my barren dreams.

Later, as we left Mike's house after the birthday fiasco, Natalie told me Tess had been Mike's nurse in the hospital, that theirs was a casual relationship to reenter Mike into the world of living, but seeing what I'd seen that night, her words yielded little peace. At least I lost the inclination to destroy *Bitter Union*, saved only by his sincere admiration.

Shattering my long reverie, Mike walked in saying Natalie was eager to see my painting, and to give her a call so we could go to lunch. I'd cleared away the plates, wiped the counter and threw the dishcloth into the sink. For some reason, his calm annoyed me, and I lashed out. "You know, you're not even prejudiced, Mike. You say all my paintings are good."

"That's because they are," he stated evenly. "Except for that pink and red thing you call *Funeral Flames*. You need to paint over that. It's a monster."

"You've become quiet a critic!"

He'd walked into the kitchen and stood beside me, putting the clean dishes into the cabinet. Now he hesitated, and a frown drew up his eyebrows almost causing them to touch each other. "First you say I'm prejudiced... Wait a minute! You're trying to confuse me." He leaned against the counter, crossing his arms and his ankles. "I never said I was a connoisseur, but I know what I like. You think it's awful, too. I could tell by the way you wrinkled up your nose, like you smelled dirty socks. But this new stuff—excuse me—these new pieces. They're airy, full of light and sensual. Of course, that's just my opinion."

The moment the words sprang from my mouth, I'd been sorry. I hung my head like a scolded child and busied myself scouring the sink. "Thursday night will tell. I hope you'll come. In spite of what I say, I value your opinion."

"This is your time, your people. Besides, I'm luckier than your other fans. I get to see you at your best, when you're giving birth."

Laughing at his metaphor, I thought, Not everything! knowing the main reason he wasn't coming: Lowell. I can't blame him. Lowell will be actively dropping names and doing the mingling bit, though not particularly good at bolstering spirits—like Mike. "If you change your mind…"

"Rhea," he took my chin and tipped my face up to the light. "I'd be out of place."

Don't beg—no matter how bad you want him there. "I don't blame you. It's all so pretentious, isn't it?" He followed me into the living room and watched me settle on the floor by the fire. "Now, are you ready to finish."

"What?"

"Oh, Mike!"

Three

"My story is very ordinary. I finished college and went to work in Dad's seafood business. A couple of years later I met Mandy at a party. She taught in the local elementary school. We dated two years and married in June 1948. Two years later the war broke out, and I enlisted. In January, 1951, I bailed out of my flak-riddled Sabre jet over Chinese occupied Seoul. Two days afterwards, I was captured."

Rhea filled our glasses, handed mine to me, took my right hand and held tight because I was already shaking violently. I had avoided talking about the past over the last months, and now facts were rolling out snatchy and stark, all I could afford.

"Meanwhile, back home, Mandy's slowly going crazy. My

family said she fought bravely for three years, wrote congressmen, called everyone the least bit involved and traveled to Washington time and again. When she collapsed, her parents admitted her to a private institution, and in a well-intentioned effort to save her sanity, they zapped anxiety and memories with electric shock treatment. A year later, her parents annulled our marriage, and she married my best friend, Trey Littlefield. When I returned, they had moved to California and were expecting a baby.

"I wondered why Mandy didn't meet the plane in Washington with my folks. They made every excuse they could: Late plane, heavy traffic.... Poor Natalie had to break the rotten news to me, and I was a raging maniac for an hour afterwards. When I calmed down, I asked question after question. Would she know me? They said yes. How could she divorce me? That's what her doctors advised. Would seeing me set her back? They told me she would be strong enough to handle our meeting; her obliterated past returned slowly so she could deal with it a step at a time. I wanted to see her, but I would have died before I would hurt her again.

"All this time, she and Trey had been waiting right outside. When she walked in, we hugged, and I felt her baby move. Strangest sensation I've ever experienced. She kept saying, 'If I'd known, if I'd only known,' over and over and begged my forgiveness. I told her there was nothing to forgive; she couldn't have known." No need to tell Rhea the part about feeling like I died inside, wanting so bad to hold Mandy, smell her hair and kiss her pale lips and not being able to fight back my tears when hers ran like rain. "I made her promise to call when the baby came or if she ever needed anything." And I'll never forget nearly coming apart when Mandy kissed me on the cheek, walked to the door, turned and said, "I'll always love you, Mike, but please understand, I've got a new life now." I wanted to let go; not feel, and have all memory zapped like Mandy's doctors did for her. Then came Trey. Under the circumstances, we did a fair job of acting normal, and parted friends. After a long while, slowly navigating my way back, I vowed to never fall in love again.

"Then they did surgery on my leg, physical therapy, and here I am." I took a deep breath and prayed Rhea would be satisfied.

She touched my arm. "Have you talked to Mandy since then?"

"Once or twice. When their baby was born. She's doing well, busy with her family."

"Mike, the letters... Would she...?"

I shook my head. "No. Besides, the letters have all been post-marked Mobile."

"What about her husband? Couldn't he have sent them to a friend, and told them to..."

"Don't ask me why I'm sure, Rhea, I just know neither Mandy nor Trey is doing this."

She wanted to see the latest. I brought them to her and she spread them over the floor, examining them intently. Shaking her head, she agreed they were from the same source—pasted on, cut out newspaper letters and words—heralding the same warnings to leave; that I'd murdered, therefore was a sinner; that I was a scourge, therefore, must be punished. Commenting on their contradictory hostile method and peace-praising, biblical theme, she reinforced our confusion by adding, "For the life of me, I can't imagine who'd want you to leave."

"Neither can I."

She teased about rivalry among my brother and sisters, and when I denied the possibility, countering they were not particularly good actors, she lapsed into unruffled but dogged interrogation. "All right, we're still no closer to solving the mystery, so tell me about the camp."

"Rhea, for God's sake!"
"Are you still having the dreams?"
"Yes."
"This isn't idle curiosity, Mike. I've read talking about recurrent nightmares will help."
"I did that with a psychiatrist."
"Did you hold anything back?"
I sighed. "Yes."
"You see. You've got to open up—one hundred percent—or the strategy won't work. Can you do that with me?"

I tossed a new log into the fireplace's gaping mouth, blew on the dying coals, and sat back. "Hope, determination… Who knows what keeps body and soul together? Early on I formulated mind games, going over and over tiny details. I spent days just thinking about Mandy's hands. I played the same game with my entire family, but Mandy kept me alive."

"Were you tortured?"

Ever since Natalie left, a steady rain tapped monotonously on the deck. With it, dampness crept into the room, and in spite of the fire, my blood turned to ice water. I could feel Rhea's eyes on my face while I stared into the trackless night and I wanted to yell, After the brutal cross examinations came the solitude combined with lack of medical attention—Yeah, I call that torture, but I answered simply, "Yes."

Compassionately, Rhea moved closer and wrapped her arms around my shoulders in her attempt to stay my trembling, but whispered, "Go on."

"I might as well start with my capture because that's what two-thirds of the dreams are about.

"After I ditched my plane and parachuted to the ground, I headed west, toward Inchon, sleeping by day, moving by night, hiding from enemy patrols. The second afternoon, two children, a boy and girl about seven and nine, were staring at me when I woke. I gave them chocolate bars, and they ran away. I followed for a little bit, intending to see if the enemy occupied their village. Soon, they brought their mother, food and water, showed me a thicket-covered cave and left. One of the villagers must have seen everything. I should have moved away instead of to—I don't know what I was thinking, but I knew I was in enemy territory. The next time I woke, six or seven rifles were pointed at my head." She pulled the woolly afghan from the sofa, draping it around us. "It gets ugly, Rhea."

"You stood it," she declared relentlessly.

"They took me into the village. I can still see women, children, and wrinkled, white-haired old men crying and running in all directions—probably fearing for their lives.

"In the center of a dirt-floored hut, they tied me to a pole. When I looked around, the family who had helped me cowered in the corner.

"First, the soldiers questioned the father, I guess. I only knew basic phrases, but he just shook his head. They hit him in the face three or four times with a rifle butt and tossed him, unconscious, aside. The woman crouched over her children, but they pulled her away, slapped her senseless then raped her while the frightened little boy and girl watched. I can still see their tiny, rag-wrapped feet gouging the dirt like they were trying to dig their way out of their hut.

"Suddenly, the young boy lunged at the soldier on his mother. The man slapped the child and literally threw him across the room. He crawled back to his sister and they covered their faces and whimpered. The father roused, tried to pull the soldier off his wife, and they shot him between the eyes. The children screamed. One of the soldiers marched over—" I gulped thickly "—lifted the little boy by the hair and chopped off his head with a machete. They did the same to the little girl. The sobbing stopped; only the mother's low wails could be heard. When they finished, they slit her throat. Nearly unconscious by this time—they'd hit me every time I moved—they carried me on the pole like a trussed animal until I came to enough to walk."

On her knees before me, weeping too, Rhea wiped my face with both her hands. "Oh, Mike, I'm sorry. I never dreamed—Do you want to stop?"

"I'm here for the cure, remember? Somebody said once, 'A topic dropped is not gone.'

"Next, came the prison camps. Blindfolded that first trip, I never knew its location. They moved me many times over the years. I believe I was behind the 38th parallel most of the time, although I couldn't swear to it.

"After my third escape attempt, they broke my right leg and didn't set it; their way of breaking my spirit, I guess, and to keep me in one place. I used a stick for a crutch during the day, binding it to my leg at night hoping the bones would heal. Life, such as it was, went along pretty good until I tried another escape. They found me, broke my leg again, and afterwards, they only let me have a crutch during the day, literally frisking me at night. By the time my leg healed enough I could get around, I'd become well acquainted with the coffin. Except for light streaming through nickel-sized air holes, I would have easily lost touch with the days. Once its lid slammed, I never knew when I'd get out."

She held up her hand. "What was the coffin?"

"A box—just the size of a person. After they brought me up the first time, I looked back, and it looked exactly like a wood coffin. Not very plush though," I chuckled. "My shoulders, buttocks and heels would go numb after a few hours.

"Ironically, the hole they dropped it in probably measured at least six feet deep, too. You'd lie down, the lock clicked, chains rattled and the box jiggled crazily on its way to the bottom.

"They fed me by pouring cold rice water, or fishless stew—I don't know what they called that food—through the air holes."

"How long would they leave you there?"

"Days became immaterial. But for the life of me, I'll never forget the first monsoonlike rain. After lying for days in my own urine and feces, while it rained, I pretended I had a bar of Ivory soap, scrubbing my skin hard. Or I'd picture myself swimming in the Gulf, later washing off the salty residue and the sticky sand under our beach shower. Mom always left sunshiny smelling towels out. In the winter, I pretended the rain was a steaming tub full of hot water. If they'd known what a good time I was having, they would have brought me up.

"But then, one time it rained for days. Nothing compares to fear of drowning when you want to live. With cold, hunger, and pain your body lets go slowly, but to drown, fully conscious, alert and unable to move while muddy, stinking sludge oozes in... That time water filled my ears, just inches from my mouth and nose. For a while afterwards, I would panic when it started raining, but then one day I decided, 'To hell with this!' and I prayed for a flood; three to five minutes, and it's all over."

"Mike, why, did they..."

"Put me there? For the first year or two, I egged them on. I had a cell mate, Rafe Lovvorn. They picked on him unmercifully. He wasn't very strong, so I baited their anger to draw them away from him. 'Godzilla,' a huge, green-toothed gook I played games with for three years, would kick Lovvorn, and I'd sock Godzilla. Notorious for breaking ribs and fingers, Godzilla couldn't get under my skin no matter how hard he tried. Lovvorn, on the other hand, whimpered continuously, sometimes to the point of hysteria. Poor Rafe. He used to tell me his grandfather, a military hero, had a statue built in his honor. His hometown even named a hotel and a street after him. Rafe wanted to be just like him and his father, who emulated his father, carrying on the footsteps of his revered ancestors. Rafe didn't last but three years. One winter, after months of dysentery and a bloody cough—he must have had pneumonia or tuberculosis—he didn't rise one morning…" I snickered. "…for breakfast. I checked him. He'd died sometime during the night. Cold and blue, they dragged him from our cell. I will say this, hopefully Rafe found peace, because his eyes definitely stared into some new, more sane place, and he was smiling. Considering his frailty, he did all right, I guess."

I loosened Rhea's fingers digging into my arm, and she apologized. "What if this gives you nightmares?" She shook her head. "Well, that's about all there is anyway, and I'm brain-dead. Oh, yeah! That's one area we lucked out in: brainwashing. Whether we escaped it because we were in a remote camp or because our captors didn't want to be bothered, we'll never know, but somehow we got bypassed. I've read it's been quite a big issue with POW's. From what we heard through the camp's message setup, I wouldn't be surprised at anything they came away saying." Rolling my head to break up the tension in my neck and shoulders, I pleaded, "Listen, Rhea, I'm exhausted. Randy and I have a charter—" I glanced at my watch "—in a few hours."

"What do you want to do with the rest of your life, Mike?" she asked lethargically.

We stared at one another blankly. I squirmed, wondering what else she wanted to squeeze out of me and fell back against the pillows, numbly focusing on the ceiling. "I'm doing it. Anyway, what's that got to do with my stamina?"

"Whaddaya think, you're over da hill or sumthin?"

I laughed. She had slipped into her Groucho, chewing sarcastic words from the side of her mouth. "S'plain to me what woiks and what doesn't woik."

"You. You work while you're not working. Do you ever sleep?"

"We got da $64,000 whiz kid here, folks."

"You're tired, too, and getting giddy. Let's call it a day."

She jumped up. Her nostrils flared, her chest heaved and I waited for the fire. "Yeah, and I can't help your lousy mood."

"Goddamnit, Rhea! What do you want? Blood?! You pressure me to tell you stuff I'm trying to forget, and then get mad when I can't entertain you all night long! You think I'm holding back, don't you? Well, I'm not. Matter of fact, you're the first one I've told half this shit to!"

"Whose fault is that?"

"I don't want your sympathy, understand!"

Placing her hands on her hips, she shoved her face close to mine. "And I'm sick of trying to help someone who enjoys wallowing in misery, do you understand? Natalie tells me you planned to be a lawyer. What happened to all your dreams? And don't tell me they went out the door with the war. I've got plans, big plans, and you're muck-sucking's wasting my time, buster!"

"Are you saying I might fit in if I'd become a lawyer? Do you honestly think I want in with that riffraff you consider celebrities? I've got better things to do, too!"

"Name one, Mr. Sanctimonious. No, let me! Spend your days improving your tan while rich old ladies paw you?"

"What do you call your cozying-up to cultural assholes? Society enrichment?"

"I paint from the heart!"

"Ah! But to what end? Fame? Wealth? I live from the heart, Rhea. Are we so different?"

"Oh, we're different, all right." She marched into the kitchen, dropped our glasses in the sink, pounded the cork into the wine bottle and thrust it into the refrigerator. "You're so nonpartisan, you're insipid. You're so afraid of commitment, you're drowning in sullenness."

All this time, both of us shouting louder and louder, I followed her around. When she whirled and headed for the door, I grabbed her arm and demanded, "What's really back of this attack?"

"Let go, Mike!" I did, and shoving me aside, she bolted. Outside, she stopped and whirled, glaring at me stonily when she saw I had followed. "You really want to know?" I nodded. "Your egocentric oblivion!"

I don't know how long I stood there. The ocean's pandemonium filled the night and my head and I had trouble thinking, but while I waited for the world to calm down she left, and I knew she was right.

Overhead, a southeasterly wind flung the clouds helterskelter, frenzied rain stung my face, so I closed my eyes. Egocentric and oblivious, huh? Well put, Rhea! Thank God for friends like you!

Staring up at her windows, I watched her pace and called up those treasured memories of our first encounter. It was one evening last fall, mid-September to be exact, and I'd sat outside admiring the day's sharp, clear colors until just before twilight. Still on crutches, I'd hobbled inside, fixed me a sandwich, opened a beer and just settled onto the sofa when she appeared in my doorway.

When she called out for Natalie, forgetting cast and crutch, I jumped up, upsetting the glass-topped coffee table and everything within the radius of my crutches. Flowers and water flew up in the air and landed on top of the sandwich that slid from my lap. Yellow beer foamed on the sisal rug, and immediately oblivious to my predicament, I almost lost touch with reality when I looked over my shoulder. Dressed in white, the sapphire night silhouetted her preternaturally, and I doubted her existence until she asked, "Who are you?" in a spellbinding, spiralling song that caused me to vibrate in its energy, its flawlessness, and male that I am, I became a mutineer. When I told her I was the tenant of this domain, amazed at the amount of fury my voice exhibited, I quickly realized she mistook Natalie for someone who didn't exist anymore, my wife. Dexterously, she snubbed my impudence and wanted to know if she might borrow a cup of sugar.

There I lay, sitting on one crutch, pinned down by a triangle of heavy glass, trying to decipher her magnetism and my anger, and she's looking for sugar! But I'll have to admit, I'd been extremely intrigued by—What I saw was not what you would call a beauty, but in a ripe-lipped, bony-jawed sort of way, provocative. Listening to her tell me she didn't use sugar, but her guests did, I quipped, "Good for you" and decided I liked her olive complexion, her smooth face, her round eyes, and her knockout body—the thought crossed my mind she might be Eurasian—and I pointed to the green canisters, telling her to help herself. I acted just like a man freed from vile years in prison and gawked at the fluid, catlike way she walked across the room, making no sound. Every detail remained etched in my mind. Light bounced from mirrored balls swinging from her ears and her hair sparkled from an unidentifiable source; when we exchanged first impressions later, she informed me the twinkle came from rhinestone barrettes. But then, she got her sugar, set the cup on the end table and started picking up magazines, my plate and the remnants of my dinner. Mesmerized, I sat there on the floor and watched, making no move to get up. Her scooped-neck dress opened to her thigh each time she bent to gather more of the mess, and silently I prayed it would come apart. For an instant our eyes locked and everything would have been all right except mine wouldn't obey. First they slid to her breasts and lazed, then they strayed to the uppermost point of the slit; here they lodged.

Anger, like a provoked rattlesnake ready to attack, flicked in her eyes, dispensing their venom, but I'd become too spoiled to care. "Obviously you're not hurt," she'd stated sarcastically.

"Only my pride," I'd confessed, feeling pretty helpless but entertained.

She stayed on long enough to help me from my entrapment, then left abruptly like she arrived. Oddly, she'd returned the next day, brought my cup back filled with sugar and a serving of the previous night's Cordon Bleu. Both of us were more sociable that time. When she inquired, nodding at my cast, if I'd had a skiing accident, I answered simply, "Nope." She didn't press, just said she'd felt bad leaving me with a ruined dinner, handing me the crushed flowers and worse when I'd said, "Thanks." The longer we talked, the more I felt like the beache's cold, sneaky rollers had smacked me on the back, shocking every molecule in me, and I wanted her to stay, and I realized what a long, long time it had been since I had seen anyone so bewitching.

Tears glistened on her cheeks when she opened the door. I apologized. Moonlight played hide and seek with the clouds, and it seemed as if she almost tumbled out, joining me in the uncompromising rain. I led her inside, found towels and threw one over my shoulder while I rubbed her dripping hair with the other. While we sipped hot chocolate, I encouraged her to tell me about her pain. She cried again, and smoothing her hair, I told her about my biology teacher in high school, Mrs. Claymore, who said, "Can't never could," when she tried that angle. Then, trying to lighten the mood, I added, "Anyway, why is it okay for you to chisel away at my saga and not tell me yours?" Nothing could have prepared me for her story. She gave in to my nagging, and later, sitting in the dark, I reeled for hours after she fell asleep.

It all began with an indulged but neglected childhood. Seeking vengeance, first she ran away from her plush Miami home, on the way out stealing a handful of her mother's jewelry. Accustomed to living comfortably, they caught up with her when she started selling it off. They placed her in a convent on the East Coast, and for a short time, she found peace. But one stormy night, her screams drowned by lightening and thunder, a workman entered her room, raped and impregnated her. Humiliated, by the time she told her parents and they consulted the priest, it was too late to have an abortion. Blessedly, she delivered a stillborn, but back at home found a new route to retaliation: drugs. This time they sent her to Europe, and this time she found comfort in art. Happy to fund her new and much more honorable passion, her parents, who she hadn't seen now for fifteen years, kept her readily supplied with cash. This she accepted, squeaking by on the minimum and banking the remainder. Before long, she started selling her paintings. A few years later and self-sufficient, she returned their checks, marking the envelopes, "Address Unknown." She moved to Los Angeles, took courses in accounting, read every proforma she could get her hands on about investments and traveled around the world for a year, selling her work along the way. From then on, she'd lived the life of a gypsy, moving when she got bored, but always keeping in touch with the trade and painting. My head swam when she told me that now, at the ripe age of thirty-four, her net worth to date tallied nearly 1.3 million.

Then she met Lowell. According to her, he took an interest in her career, and hungry for attention, she promised to marry him someday. I found this casual statement perplexing just like her epic and doubted Lowell's intentions more than ever.

Soon the sun came slinking into the sky, and she fell asleep in my arms. Manic with wanting her, I laid her on her bed and tried to sleep on her couch.

The next morning, I called Randy and told him to get someone to take my place. Rhea slept till noon. When she woke, I cooked eggs and toast and we ate, then sat on the deck swilling orange juice. She went back to bed and slept until nine in the evening. When she woke, she wanted to go for a swim. Afraid to let her out of my sight, I ran home, got my suit and went too. Back in the house half an hour later, we changed and I lit a fire. Huddling around the blaze, she seemed renewed and talkative. "You know, Mike, you pass people on the street, go for walks, live your life and have no earthly idea what's going on in anyone else's world." She rested her chin on one knee, locked her arms around it and gazed serenely at my face. "Do you realize in your own way you became an artist while you were in the camp; conjuring beauty in your head?"

How spontaneously she pulled an unreasonable situation into perspective. "Yeah, I spent days thinking about light while back home you guys were testing the Hydrogen bomb, blocking out Elvis' swivel hips on TV and making out at drive-in movies."

She laughed. Then, with the wisdom of a theologian, she spoke of spiritual strength, which I learned a lot about over the long years in confinement. Firelight flickered like an undulating dancer on the planes of her face while engrossed, I sat at her feet and listened to her story of trying Judaism, Zen and transcendentalism. "You mean like Emerson? He really had more than his share of insight, didn't he?"

"He was probably the most exalted. Thoreau, too."

"Did you join a commune?" I asked, guessing she searched not only for salvation, but acceptance and love.

"I couldn't find one!"

"I've read a bit about Zen," I volunteered. "Unstructured, individualized awareness. Intuition over rationale. Sounds like it's pretty big with the vets, too. But you know, what I really hate is I missed the Senate subcommittee hearings. Did McCarthy really nearly wreck the political system?"

She nodded sadly, and russet tongues licked sensuously up her jaw, around her lips, nose and eyes and I wanted to touch her all over. "I'm reading the Army's position right now," I added desperately. Over the last twenty-four hours I had pushed my threshold to the max and I knew I should leave, but I sat on, with her sitting there within my reach. I squirmed, amused by my selfish need and listened to her talk of peace, love, and freedom while fighting my own private battle and trying to concentrate. "What about Christianity? Did you read C. S. Lewis?"

"I tasted it all. You know what else you missed?" I shook my head. "Eating off Melamine plates with Kandinsky tendencies."

"Off what with who?"

"I think I've got some stashed away I'll pull out for you, and you still don't have a TV, although I can't say I blame you. We could teach the Chinese a thing or two about brainwashing just by watching some of our programs."

"Yeah, but I've uncovered some good stuff that happened while I vacationed in the land of the lost: Tchaikovsky's fifth, Williams' *Camino Real* and King's Civil Rights movement. Makes the unsalvageable time seem a little more worthwhile." Out of diversions, restless and not wanting to go to my cold, friendless house, I picked up my wine goblet, took a sip and fidgeted with a cushion's shaggy trim. If she knew her nearness made me crazy, she would invite me to go home immediately instead of stretching out her long legs and propping her head in her hand.

"Listen to us," she sneered. "We sound like Beatniks!"

I'd sat Indian-style, facing the fire, but my legs were going numb so I unfolded, stood and stretched, more to keep from reaching out for her than uncomfortableness and decided to test my latest notion on her. "Rhea, I'm thinking about going back—"

"Do you think a backtracking trip would end the dreams?"

"Actually, what I had in mind... Well, I thought I might adopt two Korean children. I've read there were so many orphaned by the war."

"There are lots of children here who need help, Mike!"

"But I'm responsible for the deaths..."

"Correct me if I'm wrong, but in war, death is unavoidable; living and freedom are the impetus for survival. You nor I can foresee what good comes from violence other than it gave you the will to live."

"The good old, overworked 'esprit de corps.' Rhea, a whole family died because of me! They never got a chance to voice their opinion on doctrines."

"The horrors of war!"

"Easy for you to say. You were safe..."

"Unfair! We were all scared as hell. People built bombshelters, not just to ward off Russia's threats, but to protect ourselves from our own bomb-testing, radio-active fallout and MacArthur wanting to take on the USSR!" Emphasizing her point, an angry log crashed into the ashes. Maddened sparks spit up the chimney and attacked the floor. I swatted at glowing coals. She batted my hand away, picked up her brown sandal and ground out each potential bonfire. "If you feel so strongly, go! Just don't forget, bringing Korean children to America—Would you really be helping them?"

"Meaning could they adjust? The antidote worse than the ailment?"

"Your nature is different, Mike. Whether it's from your suffering so..."

"Aw, knock it off!"

"Seriously! Do you think the average American child,

provoked by the average American parent, angered by the acrid ashes of war, will open their arms to Koreans invading their midst? Not hardly!

"Circumstance doused your hatred, Mike. And call it what you will, but a great deal of that good old 'esprit de corps' helped you get through." She placed her hand on my shoulder. "Whomever you choose, I hope they'll be deserving. Now, I know you're sick of me, and I need to shower, wash my hair and do all those girlie things, so go home, but first I want to apologize, and thank you."

"For what, being your friend? Anyway, I should thank you for your honesty."

"You may recall what Emerson said about that, 'The only way to have a friend is to be one.' We've substantiated we're good friends. Oh, yes. I'd meant to ask earlier but got sidetracked. Will you come to dinner tomorrow night? I'm having a few people in."

"Lowell?"

"No."

"What time?"

"Sevenish." She stretched her long arms toward the ceiling, rolled her head around, then let her arms dangle at her sides. Desire drew my neck tendons inches shorter than normal and I wished I could persuade her to massage them like she did one day when we sat on the beach, but I knew better than to let her touch me. She walked me to the door, and I left, the only logical action I could take without jeopardizing our friendship.

Back at my empty house, I piled wood in the fireplace, lit some kindling and waited for the heat. Intensely cold, I backed up to the flames and hunkered down. Even when she's next door, I miss her like hell, and I hope she won't leave again for a while. Watery silhouettes shimmered over the walls and furniture, and achingly lonely, I imagined myself on the brink of a black lake in the bowels of the earth, blind fish and lost souls my only companions. What if I went back? Every fragment of me wanted to! Instead, I set my imagination free and examined the prosaic monsters lurking in corners. What the hell's going on? I wondered. One fact is for sure, when I left her house I felt like all the warmth in the world stayed behind with her.

Four

The line screamed off the drag. Mrs. Dura Lazenby, of the orange and black monarch butterfly outfit, and the persistent "call me Lambie, doll" reminder, is holding on like a queen. Her shrill "Mikey, help!" finds its way into my head above the thrum of the boat's engine and Randy yelling, "Line two's hit. Line two's going. Get it, Mike!" Shit, Randy, I've only got two hands and at least one of them is batting off "Lambie" half the time! and I wondered: First of all, Rhea may be right. Secondly, is this why, back in the POW camp, I'd spend days conjuring the stained-glass light fixture over my mother's gray and red formica kitchen table? "Sit, Miz Lazenby! I'll hold it till you're in the chair."

"I wanna stand, Mikey," she whined. "You help me."

I wish Randy wouldn't run these twelve-hour, non-stop, action-packed fishing trips. As soon as we clear the pass, he wants lines out. We fish on the way out, bottom fish when we get there and bait in the water on the way home! To think I forced myself through painful memories of making love to Mandy so I'd get back! What difference did it make whether or not I could recall every word of "Stardust," the song she and I danced barefoot to in our dark apartment the night before I left for Korea? "Ma'am, you need the harness! It's a big one!"

"Oh, all right," Lambie drawled.

Christ! Why did I ever agree to do this shit for Randy? For every two turns I take, the fish takes three. Is this why I'd go over and over the silly arguments with my brother and sisters? So I could return here, my feet braced against the hull and endure Lambie's wiggling around trying to get settled? Jeez, how's she gonna…"There it is! It's a yellow, and it's a big baby!" Lambie's gonna get her money's worth in battle!

Fearing the "lady" might lose the fish, we reeled the tuna in together, and even above her thought-shredding shrieks, I speculate as to why my life pitches from serene, like the night Rhea and I walked along the beach and having her ask me how I feel when she's around, to like now, frantic. Back there is where I want to be, almost losing control when Rhea hugged me after I said, "Like all the signs are down." Was it shyness that made me keep my hands to myself, or fear of overreacting?

The next morning, I dressed for work knowing Rhea's plane should be leaving for Miami and thought, How much longer can I keep up this charade? To my surprise, I stepped out on my deck and found the twig circle with its web, beads and feathers. She'd taped it to my door with her note: "Dream

Catcher. Made by Ojibway tribe grandmother's to hang above baby's bed to filter out bad dreams, allowing only good dreams to drip from the feathers to the sleeping infant." She'd crossed out references to children and penned in my name.

Meanwhile, Lambie's whispering, "I'll make it worth your while, honey." I'm reeling like crazy and she's talking about room keys and rubbing against my shoulder and looking up at me all goo-goo eyed and not giving a frigging whit about the fish. Thirty minutes later, finishing what should have been done in twenty, the yellowfin's on board, and she's miffed because I'm helping her husband with his. We've hit a school because the other three anglers have a yellow, too. Between me and Randy, who's barking orders from the flying bridge, and three other fish, I'm whipped an hour later. Everyone's catch in, I dashed below for coffee and a donut, stuffed my hand in my cut-offs pocket and found Lambie's hundred dollar bill. I've earned it, but I'm not sure as far as she's concerned, I'm through for the evening. She kept talking about Lazzie's poker game and what she'd do to me if I did or didn't show up at her room. Is this why I practiced holding my breath in the rain until my eyeballs felt like they would pop out? Is this why I made myself exercise in the "coffin"—relax, tense, relax—to keep some muscles on my skeleton. Did I really survive to help this blitzed lady with her fish? Christ, now she's mumbling that she and Lazzie are at the Dude Ranch and asking if I know how to get there! All I want is a beer and to fall into bed, alone, at my place.

After we docked, the customer's strolled off comparing fish stories and Randy and I cleaned up the *Dizzy Dame*. Randy's counting his tip. Four hundred big ones! He handed me one, I pocketed it, looking at him quizzically when he snickered and said, "You'll come out the winner."

"How do you figure that?"

"She'll probably tip you big-time tonight."

"I'm not going, Randy."

"Why not? Who's it gonna hurt. Your not married or anything. Her old man doesn't care. Glad to have her off his case."

My little brother! Even at ten I had been grounded so long I thought my life was over because I took the blame for Randy when he set fire to a sack of dog do at Mr. Gamble's front door. It almost worked, too. Randy got away, but I'd wanted more than anything to see the expression on that grumpy old man's face when he got a whiff of what clung to his shoes. Consequently, curiosity caused me to look back, I ran into a maple tree and nearly knocked myself out. Of course, Mr. Gamble saw me and called Dad. But we're grown up now, and I don't need to worry about Randy, so I stuffed the bill he gave me along with the one Lambie tucked into my shorts in his shirt pocket. "Here. Here's your hundred and mine. I'm not going." I turned and headed to my truck.

"Mike, damnit, come back here! Be reasonable. They're good customers!"

I whirled, stomped up to my kid brother and growled, "I'm not screwing for money. Find yourself another deck hand if that's what you want!"

"Why not?" He grinned, and I wanted to sock him real bad.

"Because that's the way it is!" This time I really left. When I got to the truck I accidentally kicked my metal tackle box. It opened. Jigs and lures spilled everywhere.

Hot, sunburned and thirsty, I roared home, thinking about my conversation with Rhea that night long ago when she'd returned from her trip and found the Dream Catcher on the kitchen counter. She demanded a hammer and a nail, crawled on my bed and hung it right then and there. I thanked her and she declared, "You never cease to surprise me."

Jokingly, I asked, "When was the other time?"

The faraway look in her eyes said she took me seriously. "The night on the beach, about two weeks ago when I found you…" She hesitated, scouting my face warily.

I knew what she was trying to say so I helped her. "Crying?" Was she afraid she would embarrass me? "I don't mind admitting I've cried." But what I didn't want to discuss was the reason. That was the day I'd had the painful meeting—more like an episode—with Mandy. I feinted, trying to sound philosophical. "No one can live many years without sometime or other feeling extreme joy or sadness."

We'd walked outside, sat side by side on the picnic table and for an instant, she thoughtfully looked off at the water, but just as quickly, lifted her chin haughtily and declared, "Some people do."

The evening sun slung gold coins on the slate-colored waves and I'd seen one catch in her brimming eyes. "Not people like us. My guess is they're deceivers—to themselves."

"Frankly, I expected your usual 'yes' or 'no,' or in this case a, 'Like who?'" She leaned close, her elbows on her knees and gazed at me. Tears under control, her dark eyes held challenge when she continued. "I didn't realize you were such a student of human nature."

That's when I got a little carried away. "When time's no problem, you're free to rob and plunder insight from wherever: family, friends, and yourself. In the camp, I learned in a hurry there's all this energy, and even though you're weak from hunger, there's nothing to do but think. You're beyond dignity or discretion clouding your opinions. You search for salvation in any corner, hang to sanity by your fingernails and have plenty of time to think about principles, appraise your fellow man, and consider God."

All this time, she'd watched me closely. When I finished she asked me quite matter-of-factly what was the most important thing I had learned in life. At first I thought she stifled a laugh when I said, "That nothing stays the same," but then she got so quiet I wasn't sure whether she was shocked or just thinking.

"That's all?"

I'd nodded, reflecting on whether nearly six years of solitude had made me cynical, morose and a loner, but considering my recent lifestyle and the more recent, rocky readjustment, I thought I'd done okay.

But then she'd blurted, "You're so right." I remember the sun moved below the roof-line, dousing the room in amber, and we sat on, staring into space.

Suddenly she'd asked, "Mike, do I make you nervous. I mean…"

She'd turned away, struggling with words while I studied her profile. "No."

She looked apprehensive and meek. I remembered something she'd said about me once, and I added, "I'm comfortable with you, Rhea, and sometimes… I feel like the madness is almost gone." It worked, she grinned, and we joked for a few minutes about insanity being in family genes, so it couldn't be avoided, only helped.

But here in the present I wheeled into my driveway, jumped from the cab and inflicted my rapidly fading anger at Randy, at our clientele, and at the world on the helpless truck's door by slamming it hard. I bounded up wooden stairs that welcomed my footsteps dully telling myself I might as well get used to living in memories because more than likely Rhea and I would never share, much less dwell, contiguously in the same galaxy other than we did presently. We live in such different worlds, move in different circles and in the vastness of the universe, I knew I should be thankful for what time we've been granted, consider myself fortunate to have such a friend. Should I ask for more? I didn't want to own her. First of all, she would never allow it; secondly…What's that gawdawful smell? ...she, creator that she is, will never... Damn! What is that? ...do anything routinely. I only want her companionship. Jeeezzus! A dead skunk's at my door!

My first instinct was to kick it way out across the sand. I did, then raced around the side of the house gasping for breath thinking, Why? Who? Pushing off my sneakers, I threw them after the skunk, dashed back around and down the steps for the hose, turned it on full force and dragged it up the steps. After I flooded everything for a long time, I stripped, leaving my ruined clothes on the deck. I got Lysol, poured the whole bottle over everything and looked around, wondering what else I should do. That's when I saw, "Leave Warmonger!" painted with white shoe polish on my sliding glass door, must have passed it three or four times during the cleaning up.

Oddly, Lowell's name popped into my head. Maybe he's jealous, although I'm not sure why except I probably do see Rhea more than he does. Could he feel threatened? If so, it made dealing with the mess worthwhile! With several jobs left—to get rid of the animal and my clothes—I turned the water off and headed out to bury that damned animal. Naked, I took my shovel, walked down the deserted beach and dug a hole behind the dunes. With the skunk and my clothes on the shovel blade, I brought them to the hole, dropped everything in and covered it as fast as I could. Back at the house, I leaned the shovel against the steps and dashed for the cold water.

Filling my lungs with fresh air, I dove deep and looked around. This is the way fish feel! They don't have to breath, but I do and burst up to the surface, gulped more oxygen and dove back. I don't know how long I stayed out except I was gutter-crawling tired, and knew I should swim to the shore before I gave in to the current and let it take me wherever.

Inside, I showered the salt water away and fell into bed. I lay there in the dark facing the same, persistent questions.

Who is doing this, and why? In the camp I'd prayed to God to let me live, enough to last three hundred lifetimes. Surely He didn't help me survive to come back to this? Maybe so, because like then, after a while I got serene and slept.

When I woke, I thought the moon had snowed in my room and lay there for a long time admiring the blue-white wash before I got up. At the window, I looked up, saw it was full and laughed. I wandered into the kitchen, fixed a bologna sandwich and looked at the clock...one in the morning. Back in the bedroom, I set the clock for five, gulped the last of a glass of milk, and buried under the covers.

What if Randy fires me? He's probably thought it over and knows I'm right. If not, what the hell, I'll find something else. Besides, I've got some money, but I'll go tomorrow anyway and see.

I bolted upright, slapped the alarm clock, and instinctively wiped my forehead. It was wet. I kicked the twisted covers aside, pulled on my shorts and ran to the beach. Damn these nightmares! At the wave's edge, I stopped, lifted my head and howled at the dwindling moon like a primal animal. With the surf's haunting music at my back, I walked toward Rhea's house. It sat like a silver, heartless alien; her hollow windows, bottomless eyes.

Sometimes that gifted woman I love brings it alive, works and sleeps inside and lets me warm myself in her closeness. If she was home, I'd go to her. Sure you would, splashed a vindictive sea, but this week she's in New York having a blast! The sun turned on its power, the world's colors changed from coldly dark and mysterious to light, and soon, white and perfect, it would loosen my shoulders. Maybe then I'd forget the dreamed dirt hitting the box I'd laid trapped in moments ago, and the panic of being buried alive would seem silly. But ironically in this dream, Mandy appeared, waved and ran toward me just as the lid slammed.

Dumbfounded, I hadn't even struggled until it was too late.

Head down, I walked into the sun thinking, Things have got to get better! and they did. A sweet smelling breeze picked up and I looked around for the rain clouds. There they came, but I had plenty of time. Calmer now, I reconstructed my meeting with Mandy for the thousandth time, disputing why I went—I had no choice, what went wrong—what had I expected? No matter. None of it could be changed.

The day she'd called, I'd raced inside, grabbed the receiver, hoping it would be Rhea and shouted her name without thinking. When a hesitant but musical voice said, "Mike?" its familiarity made my heartbeat and breath stop. For a moment, a new day full of life greeted me, hope flowed in my veins and time evolved back to when Mandy stood beside me—before nightmares, before pain and before danger held dying in the palm of its hand. But with the mention of Trey and she and the baby visiting her parents, reality avenged itself. She just wanted to talk, she said. While I listened, I closed my eyes and slumped down on the sofa gripping the receiver with both hands like it was greased and might get away.

After I agreed to meet her at Sloopy's, knowing letting her in my house would be like letting her in my life again, we hung up. I must have stood in that spot for a hour listening to the aquarium hum and gurgle, watching half-bubbles float carefree on the surface. Some time calibration finally went off in my head, because I glanced at my watch without an inkling of the stretch I had just lost.

Out on the hot asphalt, I almost blistered my feet, looked down, thinking, Now I know what a beached whale feels. Panicky, I squashed nagging ideas of not going, but just as terrifying, ideas of her coming here caused me to race back and up the steps for shoes, feeling leaden and out of my habitat, too. The next thing I remembered, I sat behind my truck's steering wheel, fumbling for my keys. Back to the house. Keys in hand, this time I took a good look in the mirror and saw all I had on was my shoes and a pair of cut-off khaki shorts. Get your act together, Kipling! Mechanically, I pulled a blue tee shirt over my head, felt my stubby chin, bellowed, "I don't have time for this shit!" and stormed from the house.

On the way into town, I thought about leaving Gautier's Bay. Not only don't things stay the same, they don't get easier. Why not move to some city where friendly twilight rubs my shoulders and no one, not even the bit of fluff you sleep with for a night, messes with your life. Instead, I entered the cafe and suffered anew, noticing the cocoa colored half-circles beneath Mandy's listless green eyes. She smiled and glimpsing her thinness, I thought, Oh Lord, she's sick! Even her skin looked like only an onion's membrane of white held her deep blue veins in place.

I slipped into the booth across from her and apologized for being late. Her eyes filled quickly and I didn't want to go through this again.

"You're not late. I'm early," she said, and my own eyes stung as if I'd stared at the sun too long and burned them up.

My mouth was dry, so I asked her if she wanted a beer. She called my attention to the fact it was ten o'clock in the morning and that's when I realized it was going to be a long day. When she agreed on a coke I escaped briefly, rushed to the counter and ordered, but back in front of her, with her hair shining like the sun's own filament, I clenched my jaw when I got a whiff of her perfume—Shalimar. Did she do that on purpose?

Vulnerable, shaken and anything but clear-headed, she shocked me by asking if I remembered how happy we had been, adding she and Trey hadn't been getting along lately. Trying to change the subject, I asked about their baby, but after she told me he was growing too fast, she skipped right back to where she'd left off and wanted to know if I was happy. My better judgment told me to leave right then, but I answered, "Yes," and braced. From there on, it went down hill. She cried, said she'd better leave and I walked her to her mother's car.

First, Mrs. Wellborn's demented dog ran up, nipped my heels and I jumped inside with Mandy. Next, she told me she had left Trey, that they'd split up once before, but since I'd been found their arguments were worse. Two days ago Trey hit her, and she cried some more saying she was afraid of him now. Wishing this was all just another bad dream, I prayed to wake up, but afraid it wasn't, prayed to vanish. Instead, I agreed that she should stay with her parents, knowing I would have to leave.

Through the car's open windows, birds sang without a care, someone called, "Jimmy! Come in and wash up," my head throbbed and the soles of my feet burned. To cap the day off, Mandy's lips suddenly touched my face, searching for my mouth. Her fingers raked through my hair and crooned my name over and over. In slow motion, I grabbed her hands, but my feet were no longer on the ground, dizziness overcame me when her feverish mouth found mine, and all I could think of was Rhea. My ears buzzed, but in the distance I heard Mandy say, "I knew you still loved me." Although I'd visualized her holding me like this thousands of times, now that she did I experienced shame, and my courage returned. Finally, I'd reached the end of loving Mandy, no more wallowing in degrading self-pity. We had our time, she found another, and now it was up to me. I was tired of living in memories, tired of cowering, tired of stifling emotions, my pride raised up on its hind legs and I shouted, "I'm in love with someone else, Mandy!" No more wallowing in the bottom of a muddy hole. I'm wide awake and can deal with this nightmare!

She slapped me hard. This time when she cried I held her, soothing her trembling with gentle words, telling her I understood her hurt, her anger and sorrow. She calmed, apologized and asked who it was. I told her I couldn't say because I hadn't told her yet. Energized, she pushed away. I saw elation light her eyes like a campaigning politician ogling an overflowing war chest. Before she could start in on me again, I begged her to stop and think about it: I'd been married to her a lot longer than she'd been married to me; she got another chance; I wanted mine. I told her I'd spent the last six months forgetting the past, and I simply couldn't go back to the way things were. After a long, painful resistance, she gave in and asked me to take her home. I drove her to her parent's house and walked back to my truck.

Delilah and I raced back and forth along the beach, both chasing the stick I tossed. We kept this up until sweat soaked my clothes and I fell, panting, onto the sand. Delilah plopped down beside me, her eyes pleading for a break, too. When she washed my sweaty neck and ear with her long tongue, I got tickled and playfully wrestled her for a few minutes. We rested again, I looked into her mournful eyes and asked where she'd been when those rascals deposited their gift. I laughed out loud. Of course! It smelled too bad to get too close! After I brushed sand from her wet nose, I hugged her, telling her I didn't blame her and that I was just glad to have her put up with me.

Inside, hot and tired and closing my mind to good and bad, ups and downs, I showered, boiled a couple of hot dogs and stared hypnotically at my new television, but my mind wandered.

Randy and I have an early charter—if I'm still employed. I should call Natalie and Mom, maybe take them all to dinner tomorrow night; tonight I want to wallow. Then Rhea's words of a couple of weeks ago haunted me. "Mike, there's an old Chinese proverb, 'The Gods cannot help those who do not help themselves.' I may move to New York some day." I'd spurned the remark, vowing she loved this area too much to ever leave for good. The issue had ended right there, I'd happily maneuvered us to more pleasant subjects, but the words rattled around in my skull like seeds waiting for planting. Now's no time to think about it! Just watch *Beat The Clock* and just…don't…think, damnit!

Even my better dreams—one of which I'm having right now—revolve around times I've spent watching Rhea paint, but this time she's moving out of the room. Now we're walking down the beach. You're gone more than you're not, I'm saying, and I know I'll miss the way she tilts her head to the left when she's concentrating. Spitefully, I tell her I'm moving to Switzerland, gonna throw big parties on a balcony overlooking Lake Geneva where purple shadows soften the Alps' blinding snow just like her laughter eases my ache. She's seeing through me! and my cruelty makes me hate myself when I say, Or maybe I'll go to Africa. I'd like to feel the ground tremble when herds of giraffe create traffic jams in thick orange dust. I'll sip cognac and miss your touch. She reaches out, and I'm afraid.

No, this isn't fun anymore. I'm ready to wake up.

Who's to blame? she asks and when I let my guard down, she sneaks into my soul through my pores like osmosis.

Hell's bells, at this stage of my life, an energy-absorbing hobby like Tess is bound to be more fun! I shout.

Who are you kidding?

I'm not afraid of you, Rhea! Do you hear?

Then what are you afraid of? What you're missing?

I refuse to take part in this spoof! Wasn't it the illustrious George Bernard Shaw who said, "Your staggering vitality and endless wit will see you through, my fine man." Funny maxim. No, I certainly don't remember what it's from and what's more, I'm not sure I believe it! Now you've done it! You've made her mad!

Her head jerked around and she sneered, Go play with your dog or fight with Charlotte! Now there's a problem! Why is Charlotte so angry?

She doesn't like you! And the only member of my family that you like is Delilah. (God, I shouldn't have said that even if it is true!) Rhea lashed out at her canvas with a palate knife. I'll try to remember not to talk about them around her.

Stop! This is ridiculous! Everything's going sour. Wake up! God Almighty, Rhea! I thought you said the damned Indian thing would help!

Jack Paar's on. I slept through *Hallmark Hall of Fame*, and now that my emotional battery's charged and sleep's nomadic, I need to try and figure out who is sending these threats, smearing my car and house with fish guts and skunks, slashing my tires and breaking in my house and tumbling everything topsy-turvy? And you know what else, Buddy? You might as well practice living life without Rhea or else pray like hell—it's worked before.

At dusk two days later, I saw a light on in her studio. I knocked and she appeared, red paint smeared on her left jaw, hair recklessly pinned up, and wearing that long, once white, paint-smudged shirt that always reminds me of the biblical one Joseph wore. Reeking of turpentine, she rubbed a brush into a cloth, glared at me and scolded, "You can't come in now. I'm busy." Bitterly disappointed, I swallowed the words about to explode from my mouth, how she couldn't have looked prettier if she had just stepped from a beauty parlor. Instead, I smiled and left, her curt words ringing in my ears and my scalp crawling with rejection.

A week passed. Early Sunday morning, Delilah and I trotted along the sand toward the still blurry west and Rhea slipped up behind me, asking, "Are you avoiding me?"

Tired of missing her and ready to take my chances, I answered cautiously, "No, just busy."

She smiled suspiciously. We ran side by side in silence until all at once she dropped back. I whirled around and ran back to where she stood, doubled over. "Are you okay?"

"Out of breath; out of shape. Let's rest a minute," she gasped, pointing to a nearby dune.

Ignoring the biting wind, we huddled atop a mound of sand surveying the deserted beach. Her closeness hurt. I wanted to ask how the painting was going, if she'd spend the rest of her life with me but instead I sulked, fearing she'd reprimand again. Finally, she admitted the wind was going right through her so we rose and skidded down the knoll. At the bottom, she grabbed my arm. "Mike, what are you brooding about?"

"Nothing."

"This is me, Rhea. 'Nothing' isn't good enough. Fess up."

After several of my unconvincing denials, she said, "Sometimes, if I'm distracted, I never recapture the absolute worth of that moment again." She stared at me for a long time. "I've hurt your feelings, and I'm sorry, but you must remember artists are notoriously temperamental. Whatever I say or do that sounds ridiculing, remember I'd never jeopardize our friendship intentionally. My honesty sometimes reeks of sarcasm, which is a flaw in my personality, but to you—Well, just remember, it's not meant personally. You mean too much to me..."

"Hey, enough!" I grabbed her, pulled her close and held tight, wondering why I stopped her from saying what I wanted to hear. What better opening could a guy ask for, but I didn't want her groveling because I'd acted childish. Encouraged, I held her away and smiled, knowing we had connected like never before.

"So, do you think you can sit and watch quietly if I let you return?"

Like a kid promised a trip to the circus, I replied eagerly, "I'll be good, I swear!"

Five

I shut the box and thumbed through yesterday's mail: the gas bill, this week's *Time*, an offer from *Reader's Digest* and another legal-sized, parchment envelope. They're coming more often; the last just three days ago, another the week before. Back on the drive, I picked up the *Press Register*, tucked everything under my arm and headed up the blacktopped road to the house. At the steps, I sat and turned the menacing envelope over and over. Same as the others. My name, no return address, postmarked Mobile. I tapped it against my palm and tore a narrow strip from the end. Inside was the usual folded sheet of watermarked paper. Crudely cut-out letters formed the words, "EVIL HAUNTS FALSE HEROES."

Another with almost a biblical ring, but on the next line a genuine threat: "LEAVE BEFORE IT'S TOO LATE!"

The urge to look around was overwhelming. Did the culprit lurk behind a dune enjoying my bewilderment? No one in sight, but what did I expect? The beach is almost deserted this time of the year. I looked at my watch. Time to head for the harbor and see if I have a job. I'm acquiring quite a stack of these warnings although I'm no closer to knowing what I've done and who I'm bothering. Before this last one, there had been others declaring, "THERE'S NO ROOM FOR YOU HERE! and "GO BACK TO THE GRAVE!" and "NEXT TIME YOU MAY NOT SURVIVE!"

A frigid, hostile breeze fluttered the paper in my hand and I shivered. I rose, crossed the deck and leaned on the rail. The ocean's beauty trapped me. Pale green and smelling salty and fresh, wisps of vapor scudded across its surface like low flying clouds, or better still, some wayward spirits scurrying to arrive home before good daylight. What made the water so soothing? Did we really evolve from subterranean depths? Is the desire to return to our origin so great, even after millions of years, its nature calls us perpetually?

Inside, I grabbed my jacket and keys. On the way to my truck, I stole another quick look. With a little luck, soon I'd be beneath this brilliant sky, slicing through sparkling waves—but on the other hand, my eyes would be glued to whomever we took out; watching for careless, unleashed hooks, rigid lines and listening to loud bragging. More often than not, our customers paid little attention to the ever-changing magnificence of the cloud formations, the water shifting to richer colors with its depth, the sly, babbling birds following for scraps or tipping us off to schools. Even the noble creatures we landed, fighting to the painful end, were incredible; such iridescent, rainbow colors, such strength, but so defenseless against determined man. I looked at the smokey color hanging just above the horizon. Later today, when the white sun reached its peak and hung lifeless in a bleached out sky, heat sapped energy would flow from my pores, and I'd have to baby everyone into drinking lots of fluids.

At the pier, Randy nodded and grinned. The turkey! He knew I'd be back. Despite our tiffs, I like working with him, and except for dealing with paid-for attitudes, I like going out, and he knows all this.

We got everyone on board, settled in and left the harbor. In the channel the wave tops flashed silvery, and I thanked God for letting me live; I just wish I had some clue why anyone would begrudge me the privilege.

A gray and white gull hung suspended in the clear air. He dropped, caught the wind under his arched wings, flapped and glided out of sight, screaming a soulful farewell. For some reason, I wanted to share this sight with Rhea. She's probably up by now, smearing oil paint on her canvas and never guessing since I'd met her my life's not been the same.

The boat's quiet. Everyone's more interested in cradling cups of Randy's steaming coffee than fishing. While I've got time, I rack my brain. I know so few people with the exception of my family. After almost six years in that damned, stinking hole, at times holding on by a slowly fraying thread, whose life had I messed up by coming back?

Since my visit with Mandy, and long before Rhea's hinting, Trey's name had bobbed up again and again like the cork of a teased fishing line. If Mandy told him why she left... Or maybe he thought I'd encouraged her... Certainly his chances of getting his life back to normal would improve if I'd stayed dead. Maybe I should call him. It might make him feel better if I told him about Rhea. I'd better watch out, though. Before long, so many people will know—not necessarily her name, but that wouldn't be too hard to figure out—she'll be the only one who doesn't.

But I hadn't totally eliminated Lowell as a suspect either, and if it is him, I'll have another problem. Rhea won't stand still while we battle it out, and fight I will if he's the one! However, if I follow through with a promise I've made to myself—to leave if Mandy moves in with her parents—and if Rhea moves too, it will all resolve itself.

All day long worthless questions flooded my head: Why did Trey and Mandy move to California? I heard he didn't have a job when they went out. Had he loved Mandy all the time? If it is Trey or Lowell, why don't they just step up and say so? If I do leave, and Mandy's with her parents, how will that improve Trey's life? So that leaves Lowell. He stands to lose more financially and emotionally, but I've never seen any indication Rhea really loves him or I wouldn't be crowding his turf so, therefore, his motive could only be founded on rivalry.

The peculiar thing here is no one seems to take into account I've suffered a loss, too, except for my family. Certainly they aren't candidates. I guess that's why I haven't mentioned the letters or the incidents to them. Except for Rhea, they still know more than anyone else about my bad luck. They saw my heart breaking when Mom said, "We've lost touch," after my asking, "Where's Mandy?" for two hours. When they finally did tell me, I'd looked over at Dad and all I could think of was him saying, "Keep it right side up and between the ruts," my motto every time I'd almost run out of faith. So it must be Lowell.

Delayed by engine trouble, we docked late and finished stowing gear even later. Bone-aching tired, I drove home, popped a beer, and although I was weary, I fidgeted and couldn't relax. I dragged out the patio broom. With the contrast of black asphalt and white sand my guide in the murkiness, I swept back the granules gobbling up my driveway.

Back on my deck, a chill ran down my back, and I chuckled. Another one of Dad's sayings, "A rabbit ran over your grave," came to mind. I dropped into the canvas hammock, closed my sun, wind and occupational-hazardously strained eyes and listened to the undulating waves slosh out on the beige sand, hoping their serene sound might soak up the tension in my spent muscles.

Overhead a thick sky tinted the same yellow of our malaria-infested skin hung ominously. The color registered important—storm brewing?—but I'm too concerned about the hollow raps echoing in my ears to dredge up the significance. The jungle's lush foliage brushed against my cheek, and I froze, its dampness a knife in my blood. Close to my right eye, a droplet of water quivered on a leaf. I looked through it and saw eternity sucked into its transparency without me, and I knew deep fear.

The rapping grew louder. The long stick I used for a crutch dug into my armpit's flesh. If only I had two good legs. I took a wobbly step. A twig snapped. I held my breath and muttered, "Damn," but it was too late. A dirty, brown hand brushed aside the limb, and standing dead-center in my path, I looked into a gook's flat, squinty eyes.

A silly grin cracked open the green-streaked face, revealing large, protruding teeth. The gray cap and the tightly buttoned tunic flashed "Enemy!" to my brain. The rifle clasped across the gook's chest rose and charged toward my face. Hold on! I screamed silently to my brain, but the butt of the gun crashed into my forehead. I toppled backwards, lost my balance and fell through the brush. A blow to the gut. Another, and I gasped for breath. Sharp pains raced up my leg. Hot bile rushed up my throat, and I blacked out. With a thud I'll never forget, the solid wood door slammed and I came to on the dirt floor of my cell. Eddie helped me to my mat—he hadn't made it either—and I turned away, swallowing my pain-choked sobs and concentrated on raising my private, protective wall.

Suddenly, I'm naked, climbing over a barbed-wire fence. The beach lies ahead, and I ignore the rips in my flesh and scramble over. People are staring, but I hear the waves slapping against the sea wall and I've made it to the top. Freedom! Somehow I know it's mine and I fill my lungs with clean, pine scented air. But then there's an explosion and my body breaks up. Parts fly through the atmosphere. I'm on the sand scrambling around to find my arms and legs but don't have any hands. Bobbies—the kind that guard the Queen's palace—with fuzzy black towers on their heads, screeching whistles in their mouths and shiny wooden sticks—they have my hands!—grab me and pull me along—that one has one of my legs!

Muffled footsteps pounded down the hall, the room shook, and a voice broke through my agony. "Mike!" Half-expecting to see narrow, mean eyes and big, dirty teeth, I shook myself awake and looked around. Instead,—Thank God!—Rhea stared through the screen door. Happy to see her familiar jet eyes, tan face and dark brown hair, the sand, the ocean, everything! I watched her open the door and glide toward me. "Are you okay?"

Still trembling, I ran my fingers through my damp hair, and wanted to scoop her up and fly away to the mountains on a expedition of some sort. I almost asked her if she'd come, but I'd been holding my breath and gasped. "Yeah. Dozed off, I guess." My heart beat loudly in my ears. Calm down, you ass. "Want some coffee?" Green leaves, grass and sloping hillsides. We could sleep on the ground and listen to the noises of the forest. Hmmm.

"No thanks," she answered softly. "Mike, you jumped clear of your chair. Were you having a nightmare?"

"No!" I snapped, immediately sorry. My temper shortens with each of her departures and I don't know why but it doesn't improve much with her returns. I laughed. "I mean yes, but it was a daymare."

"Then I'm glad I woke you."

In spite of being relieved by her presence, I didn't want to talk about the past and searched frantically for a suitable topic. "Want to go to the pottery tomorrow? I've got the day off." She passed me, floated into the kitchen and poured herself a cup of coffee. She looked over her shoulder and grinned. "I changed my mind. You make such irresistibly delicious smelling coffee." While she moved about getting a spoon, pouring milk into her cup and replacing the bottle in the refrigerator, I pasted a smile on my mouth, devoured her with my eyes when she wasn't watching and waited. Back on the porch, she said, "Sure. What time?"

"Make it easy on yourself," I mumbled, getting a whiff of her obscenely seductive fragrance. "White Shoulders" she'd told me one night, and all of a sudden I know I can't do this friendship shit much longer! I want to drag her into the bedroom... "Have you painted today?" I asked nervously, staring at her golden profile. Humph! What difference did it make? The feelings need to be mutual before it'll work.

"I've been hard at it since four o'clock this morning. I needed a break."

This time of the day always made her look like one of Matisse's native girls, sans bright sarong. "I guess so. The sun's going down." Today she wore her usual: white shorts and a long-sleeved, thin white shirt. Damnation! Doesn't she ever get cold? She should wear more clothes, although I'm burning up. Maybe I'm catching a cold.

"Want to come see?" Her eyes went all round and proud like a child's.

"Sure." I wish she'd wear something bright and go topless.

Maybe she'd like to go for a swim. Hoping she couldn't read my mind, I followed her down the steps and headed for the dune that separated our houses. The sand squeaked beneath our sneakers as we trudged up the mound. Going down, we dug in our heels and she squealed when she slipped. Not going to help her up. Can't touch her! When we got to her steps, we stamped our feet, leaving a fine dusting on the threshold.

"The light's not right on one face, but—Oh, you'll see."

I stared at her back, knowing beneath her loose shirt snaked soft olive skin. One night, in a new breed of dreams, I'd lain at her back, kissed her shoulders, and while she'd slept I'd traced the tiny ridges with my fingertip thinking she's so thin I can almost count the vertebrae. Then I'd turned her over and moved to the perfect, white triangle outlining that shadowy jungle obscuring that addictive corridor, waking her…

"What do you think?" She stood beside a large canvas covered with bright colors, watching and waiting, and I wanted to evade reality, not leave that delicious dream that let me patronize her, administering lingering kisses. Up, up to the other white island, a narrow ribbon crossing her heart. There, two lofty peaks each pinnacled by a blunt, rosy nub, grew rigid when brushed back and forth with my tongue. Stop this, for chrissakes! but I'd kissed them and…"It's—it's fantastic," I stammered. "When did you do all this?"

"I told you. The canvas was empty when I got up."

While she talked excitedly, I paced the room. Fighting discomfiting arousal, I rummaged around in my head for a distraction only to recall Natalie's comments after she'd first met Rhea. "Good luck keeping your life private." While the movers were bringing in my things, Natalie had encountered Rhea, afterwards telling me Rhea commented on the diverse mixture of modern and antique furniture. But Nat's vivid summation of Rhea's features was what intrigued me: "You neighbor's different. Always in flowing white. Big eyes and mouth—almost too big—for sort of a dainty face. Tall, dark complexion, and makes strange comments like, 'I work at night.' She may be a prostitute."

"That'll work," I'd wisecracked.

Natalie huffed, "Men!"

But time passed, and Natalie's speculation turned into just that. Rhea is different in that she denies owning a last name, does keep odd hours, and is impatient with everything except painting. And I honestly believe she knows what I'm going to say before I do, but the best part of all is, she's just Rhea, and I'm pretty sure we're far from being enemies.

Now I could only blink, watching her brightly painted mouth, listening to her critical review of her painting and wanting to shake her skepticism free, my soul fervent in the belief a genius stood before me.

Some days she'll even let me watch her paint, and I'm fast learning her idiosyncrasies. When she's concentrating, she'll tilt her head to the left, step back and chew on her brush's stem. Most days she knows what she likes and dislikes, but I've seen her cautious daubs, and I've seen her lash out in long hard strokes and turn the whole blessed mess into mud.

The first time I saw her destroy one of her paintings, I wanted to jump up and shout, "Have you lost your mind?!" Thank goodness, I didn't. The next time, I'd thought what nice trees and people and I did ask warily, "Why did you do that?"

She peered at me with narrowed eyes. "Did you like it?"

"I thought it was nice."

"Ah, nice," she whispered wickedly. "Then I did the right thing." She'd turned and started cleaning her brushes, and right then and there I decided I'd better keep my opinions to myself.

But now, she's picked up a brush and applied a dab of crimson to a leaf, following with pale green on a brow, magically supplying dimension. A stroke here, a touch there and her scenes, although sometimes unidentifiable to me, take on life.

Busy creating, she's forgotten I'm in the room. To keep from distracting her, I looked around for her newspaper, but that would be too noisy. On the littered coffee table, I noticed an open book, picked it up and saw the title, *Vanished Cities*. I yearned to ask if she's planning another trip, but bit my tongue, not wanting to put ideas into her head. She had stopped at page 43—Pompeii, and I prayed that isn't where she's having her next exhibit. Too far from home, and me. Keeping her place with my finger, I flipped forward, then backward, thinking I'd go with her if she asked, but deep down inside, I know we aren't working out the way I'd hoped. Friends, yes, but I longed for more.

For the next hour, I read captions beneath pictures of fossilized ramparts, stew-pot shards, and a bronze head unearthed in 1754 with the discovery of a city called Herculaneum. It says here the city was destroyed by a thick cloud of ash and gas, sending the population running frantically toward the sea. Nipping their heels, a broad wave of pumice and rock fragments liquefied by 750 degree Fahrenheit temperature enveloped Herculaneum. Its villagers died in a hot grave belched from Vesuvius, trapped in flight, encased in stone or asphyxiated in a cloud of smoke.

Feeling a strong sense of déjà vu, I glanced from a page to Rhea's canvas. There, unexpectedly, in an outdoor dining room complete with fountain, lounged a wealthy Roman whose clone filled a third of Rhea's canvas. Intrigued, I turned pages rapidly. Here were similarities between the nature scenes in Rhea's park and Pompeii's unearthed floor mosaics. In another scene, she's captured old-fashioned rose bushes hiding a bobcat, its extended claws holding a prehistoric nightingale. But Rhea, now painting furiously, never stopped to refer to the book. Ambling around the room, I flipped through stacked canvases. Amid her pale humans—which I suddenly realized were more like shrines—these unorthodox goings-on lurked, hid and peered. My God! She's on a trip all right, right into the past.

Feeling unpolished and uneasy, I rose, consoling myself with the promise of her company to the pottery tomorrow, and silently slipped outdoors. I strolled the moonlit beach, tossing sticks for loyal Delilah to retrieve, drifting from threadbare passion to ironclad moodiness. All I wanted—Yeah, yeah, we know what you want. But what about Rhea's needs? I'm prepared to make huge sacrifices. Do you two have enough in common? If she'll just love me a tenth of what I feel for her… Are you willing to sit by while she flits all over the world? Sure! As long as she comes home to me! Can you convince her this is what she wants? Somehow I will.

God, I'm hot. And I feel so weak. I think I'll go home, eat a bite—but I'm not hungry—and just go to bed.

Six

What I thought would be a spring shower turned into steady sheets of cold rain and lingering, dingy clouds—remnants of an unseasonable tropical storm—so I painted. Mike sounded disappointed when he called, saying "Guess we'll have to postpone our trip to Sheerwater," but I jumped at his secondary invitation to dinner, the first indication of "cabin fever" I'd noted.

Now, I'm worried we're teetering on the edge of our own magnetic storm. Tonight, when he opened the truck door, I passed him stepping into the cab, and sniffed Old Spice, discreetly applied but undeniably present.

People use you. Did you know that? You thought it was

your engaging wit and intelligent conversation, right? Wrong! I bet you thought they were interested in you because of… What?…your good looks, your new car, money, your availability at a moment's notice. You're getting warm. And another thing I've learned, no matter how fast you run, life's going to catch up with you with all its sweetness and vileness—thank God there's a mixture or we'd all take a walk into the ocean.

But back to people—let's be nice and call them friends. In my younger days, I guess I strove for recognition, sometimes telling outrageous lies—Did you know when I was fifteen I was dying of an incurable cancer? Guess what? That scares the hell out of people, so don't use that gimmick. But just in case you don't believe me, try it. Folks will run like their coattail's on fire (I read that cliché somewhere, and it's pretty close to true!). The weather is fickle, but a friend, and many times a close relative—Beware!

And did you ever notice when it comes to things that are monumental to you, and you try your best to let someone know you care what happens to them, they go off and die and no one calls to let you know? You find it out at some insignificant party you started not to attend or over casual conversation—years later! Doesn't it make you question where peoples' heads are?

Have you ever needed help, or a good ear to tell your troubles to? Look in the mirror and tell them to yourself and you'll get better results! Psychologists say, "You're your own worst enemy." I say, "You're your best friend!" Trust me!

Learning this the hard way and dedicated to my analysis, I've trained myself to need no one and be skeptical of friendships. You may think this callous, but I say whatever a person finds works best for them, do it! I'm not saying I'm not open to sentiment or other viewpoints, and what happened almost six months ago proves this. I met Mike, the downfall of all my postulating and my heart checkmated my hard-fast rules. Denial ruled my head for quite a while after I'd opened his door, seeking Natalie, and faced a thin, bushy-faced, and obscenely bold man who peeled my body nude with his wild-animal eyes. I recoiled. There was no courteous, false preamble in his voice, his mannerisms or his body language. Every fiber of his being radiated anger, and on closer observation, something near madness. It had been a long time since I'd feared another human being, not since a mugger knocked me down and stole my purse on a brightly lit New York City street. To that, I'd chalked awe up to the unknown—I never saw the attacker's face. But the first time I saw Mike, totally incapacitated—cast on one leg, sitting on his crutch, and a thick wedge of glass practically in his lap—I'd been that frightened again. The next day, I returned the borrowed cup of sugar and took him some leftovers from my soiree the night before, partly out of curiosity, but ninety-nine percent to check my grit. I'd been right, although this time, I detected the slightest crack in his fierceness.

Months later, when he'd cleared his face of the cinnamon-colored brush, smiled genuinely and the eyes softened, I relaxed too. Of course, after gleaning some of his secrets from his sister, Natalie, and gouging what I surmised as sketchy details from him, I'd empathized with his first impertinence.

Through all this, I've never noticed him wearing aftershave or I wouldn't be so surprised right now. Is it as significant as I deem? Is our friendship about to end? I hoped not. I could always say, "No, Mike, let's keep things like they are," if he tried to kiss me.

On the drive into town we discussed the startling find of the Dead Sea Scrolls. He'd asked if I thought this would outshine the ancient quest for the Holy Grail? And would Judaism and Christianity accept a "new" spiritual message, if such were uncovered? Together we speculated about what happened to the Bedouin shepherd boy who stumbled upon the caves and the texts, contemplating whether or not fame changed his life.

Inside the restaurant, he ordered, and I ate ravenously. Earlier, when the phone rang, I'd been gulping orange juice from the bottle and eyeing curling slices of pink ham. I'd painted all day and the apple and chunk of cheese I ate that morning were used up. But the abstract that I titled, *Jewels By Night*, flowed easily up the canvas, with what I perceived to be a cleverly employed strategy: monochromatic, foreshortening my masqueraded people to the point of distortion, and implementing Bierstadt's ethereal back-highlighting. Once, I even thought I smelled the city's sour streets, and heard the wicked laugh of my trollops from the black alley. When I told Mike the painting spoke, he hadn't laughed. Instead he said he believed me, and that when they were out on a charter he could smell atmospheric changes and even where fish lurked. In the background, I saw Lowell grimace and give my painting his own interpretation that would sound something like, "A brilliant contemporary artist's translation of—" ticking off none of the things I'd so succinctly concocted. But then Lowell possessed the most bland imagination of any man I've ever known. Light meant nothing except to bring out the best on my paintings; shadows, he tried to avoid; depth meant thickness of paint on the canvas. But no doubt he could persuade the most tight-fisted art lovers to buy, whether for investment purposes or real love of beauty. Contrary to my constant scrambling to maintain my individual techniques and flee his formula explanations, I still wasn't sure why I'd agreed to marry him. Weak moment, I guess.

But earlier, when I invited the incredibly uncanny Mike to come in and tell me what he thought, he took one look and said, "Those women—your jewels—are afraid, aren't they?" Speechless, I nodded, and he added, "You've sure captured evil in those shadows, and I like the way you've got the light coming from behind." I wiped my brushes, dropped them in the jar of turpentine, intending to clean and put them away when I returned and stepped back, contemplating my day's work in a new light. While I'd waited for him, I had eyed the painting analytically and rated it clichdic and bleak, but now I couldn't bring myself to obliterate it without killing something of Mike's solidity. Thank goodness he would never say things like, "nice blocks of red, yellow, etcetera, etcetera," and although this might never sell, I swore to myself it would remain untouched.

I asked him once if he'd ever taken art and he laughed. "Yeah, but I got an art major to help me pass." That I can visualize: some trembling, petite hand holding his, guiding the brush strokes and with downcast eyes, grilling him on perspective, the color wheel or shading techniques.

So why don't I want this nice person to kiss me? I like him. He's handsome in a rugged sort of way. And tonight he smells good. Most likely, it would be delightful!

What is he thinking now? He looks a little pale. Certainly quiet, not eating much, just watching with pleasure while I gulp my thick hamburger.

He edged from the booth, sauntered to the gargantuan, dome-shaped jukebox, dropped in some coins and punched several buttons. Jo Stafford's haunting voice crooned, "Fly the ocean in a silver plane..." The phantasm's bubbly neon effervesced an unearthly blue around Mike's body as he walked toward me, and I chuckled, thinking he looked like something from outer space. "Just remember till you're home again..." Between broken giggles, I tried to describe this comic book scene to him, but he dropped onto the seat across from me, gripped his Miller's with both hands and his whole body drooped. I wanted to kick myself; but on the other hand, he'd been looking too serious. Don't worry, he'll not try to kiss you tonight, smarty. "Oh, Mike," I snickered, and burst into a new round of laughter. "Confinement," I vowed. "I get like this whenever I'm snowbound, too." Knowing he selected that song especially for me, and trying to salvage his miserable frown, I squeezed his hand while Jo harmonized "...pyramids along the Nile..." and impetuously, I blurted, "Hey, let's dance!" I never meant to say that! Freudian slip? Probably.

Rather nonchalantly, he rose and held out his hand. Gingerly, he placed one hand at my waist and held the other like it was fine china. We took two steps and the song ended. "Oh, well. Guess we might as well head home. Lowell is supposed to call." I thought I'd quit doing stupid stuff like that in college! "Of course, he should be busy, busy cementing details for my fall show in Paris." I turned and headed for our table.

"Pretty exciting, huh?" Mike mumbled woodenly to my back.

"Yes." I sat down, and hoped Lowell would call while I was out, but instead of having the good time I'd like him to suspect, I'm busy, busy making a fool of myself. What a klutz!

The waitress cleared the table and asked if we wanted another beer or dessert. I replied I was fine, but Mike ordered another beer, and I worried about the aftershave again. Awkward silence. Didn't he hear me say I needed to leave? I plopped my purse on the table and squirmed. More cold silence. When I asked if he'd seen any of his family lately, he answered, "No," rather brusquely, and I wished I'd stayed home. Gallantly, he asked when Lowell would be back and I looked up, but he looked away. He's uneasy. I'm not sure why, but I know he's trying to salvage the evening. "Tuesday or Wednesday," I answered. "I'm not sure." He'd punched the button for "Sincerely" too, because we were the only ones in the diner except for a shabbily dressed, heavily bearded old man chain smoking, and hunched over the table nursing a cup of coffee, no doubt seeking comfort for his hangover. The Andrews Sisters' tinny voices filled my ears and I wondered why we're having so much trouble finding something to talk about. What's wrong? His mood or mine?

"How did you end up in Gautier's Bay?"

I think he's stalling! He's not ready to give up on the evening, and I watched more closely. "Because of the pottery."

He brightened. "Pottery?"

"Remember? That spot east of the harbor we'd planned to visit today?" He threw back his head and laughed. "What's so damned funny?"

"You and pottery. If you'd said, 'Some rare pigment only found in local creek banks,' I'd have understood."

Reminding him of my collection, he looked like I'd told him I found Amelia Earhart's plane in the Pacific, nodding kindly. I felt compelled to explain how sometimes, having painter's blah, I traveled around looking for additions to my assortment, usually coming home with new earthenware and fresh images to paint. "So what if I've fallen for the beach, the picturesque fishing village—or whatever it is everyone here does. Besides, it's not too far from New Orleans, Mobile and Jackson, cities that are beginning to take some interest in local artists."

"But you stayed."

"So? Maybe I've run out of space and potteries."

He laughed softly, and I asked if he'd been to the pottery. "Oh, yes, but not for a long time."

His sleepy smile remained. I ducked my head and peeked at his lowered eyes. "Pleasant memories, huh?"

"Yes."

"Oh, come on! You're dying to tell me!"

"Well, it was on Halloween night. I was in the eighth grade." I snickered. "I told you it was a long time ago!"

"Go on. I promise not to laugh."

"You'll laugh. I got my first kiss there—on a scavenger hunt."

"Was that on your list?"

He chuckled and looked at his beer bottle like it had turned into an Arabian belly dancer. "No."

"Was she pretty?"

"Oh, yeah," he answered, his voice silky, his eyes dreamy.

"My goodness, Mike. What was her name?" I held my breath, knowing it must be Mandy. No! He'd not met Mandy until after college.

"Barbara Ann."

"What happened? Did you date?"

"As dates go. Dad drove us to serious stuff, like dances. We walked to the movies, held hands, did a lot of kissing out back..."

"Out back of what?" I leaned close, watching this quaint recollection maneuver over his face. I wanted to know, but more, I wanted him back.

"The school, her front door, the trees, you name it, we kissed there."

"My, my. How special. I'm almost afraid to ask..."

"Oh, no. Our folks would have killed us."

"So... What happened?"

"We just sort of drifted apart." He looked up. "You're enjoying this, aren't you?" I nodded eagerly, he slumped deeper in his chair, and a faraway look came into his eyes. "Nothing quite like that first kiss. You never know that tenderness again." He straightened, picked up his change, took the last long swallow from his bottle and I watched his Adam's apple slide up and down, thinking, Nice, not sharp like some men's.

He left the waitress a healthy tip for not much service and totally convinced he's an old softy, I'm more amazed than ever that he did survive all those years in a POW camp. "Now," he said, taking my arm and leading me outside. "Your turn."

With his arm around my waist—Watch out! That's a first—he pulled me along down the street, but then he let go, and I thought, He's probably going to try to hold my hand. Why not? I waited, but he didn't. He stayed in step, glancing my way expectantly. Lifting my face to the starry sky, and searching my memory, I began my story. "We did it in a front porch swing. One hot, humid summer's night in Charleston after my parents went to bed. Otherwise, it was nothing phenomenal."

Expecting more questions, I glanced his way. The shadows hid his face, but he'd jammed his hands deep into his pockets. "I thought you grew up in Miami."

He thinks I lied! No. He isn't watching me. It's more like he's trying to… What the hell! Is he going to turn out like all the rest, reading what he wants to believe into my words! On the defensive, tempered with borderline exasperation, I braced, hoping he'd have sense enough to tread lightly! "Every summer we visited. Mom's old maid sister, Aunt Emelia, lived there."

"So what did you think of your first kiss?" We passed under a street light and I saw his eyebrows were lifted like I'd seen him do before, in that curious, cunning way he has, making them almost touch in the center of his forehead. "Come on now, Rhea. I told you!"

"It was awful. Wet, slippery, tangled arms, a dozen or so, and bumping noses. We talked about doing it for half an hour beforehand, and I'd about gotten out of the mood."

His laughter rolled deep in his throat. "But you didn't give up?"

"No. We finally did it. Afterwards, I remember contemplating what the big deal was."

"How old were you?"

"Eight or nine. I don't remember."

"Jesus! I'd always heard girls were faster than guys. What then?"

"Nothing. We both just wanted to do it, so we did. His name was Larry something or other. Nice blue eyes and red, curly hair—you know, like those plastic scrubbing pads—and a million freckles all over his ears, his eyelids and…"

"Yeees"

"I would imagine everywhere. I saw him around several summers afterwards but we never really dated. Aunt Emelia said he went to Law School, became a Democratic State Representative and all that fine statistical stuff. Wife's family is upstanding, three or four freckled-faced, red-headed brats, I suppose. I do remember my family was highly disappointed I didn't hang onto him."

"Rhea, surely you've wanted to get in touch with your folks?"

My head snapped around, my anger flared red-hot. "Why? Because they'd be proud I've become a self-supporting, mildly popular artist? That would make them look good. I've made it on my own, and they're not going to bask in the sunshine of my achievements. They don't care, Mike! Anyway, I'm tired of this topic."

"Fair enough. Do you still want to go dancing?"

"After you answer one for me. Earlier, when I mentioned Charleston, I struck a nerve didn't I?"

"Not much escapes you, does it? Mandy and I honeymooned there. We… It's a nice town."

Wishing I'd obeyed my gentler instincts, I muttered, "Yes, it is."

Surrounded by rows and rows of cars, the "Tally Ho's" roof flaunted a blinking blue neon horseman in pursuit of a blinking red fox. When I stepped from Mike's truck, I felt the music pulsing in the ground beneath my feet. Ready to change my mind, I grabbed his arm and whispered, "I haven't danced in eons."

"It's like riding a bike."

Inside, there wasn't room to try his theory, much less dance. All the couples on the floor were doing was swaying, their heads hidden in thick blue smoke that rested eerily on their shoulders. We sat at a tiny table crammed between two others and I ordered a Whiskey Sour, Mike, another beer. Above the music's din, we yelled at each other once or twice, and giving up, Mike nodded toward the floor. We rose and stood on the fringes of the crowd. He took my hand and worked us deep into the spellbound mob. He faced me, pulled me closer, and suddenly, the crowd surged and pushed us together. His right leg slipped between mine, my breasts mashed against his hard chest, and I tensed. He drew back and looked at me and said, "This isn't much fun, is it? Wanna go?" I nodded and we wove our way to the door.

Outside, his hand touched the center of my back, urging me aside and I thought his touch seemed hot. Two twittery couples rushed by and vanished into the thundering swell. We climbed into his truck. Soon, in wintry silence, we bumped down a back road and I wondered where he was going. Surely he wouldn't! That's what teenagers would do!

"How did you meet Lowell?"

Before I could respond, headlights illuminated the cab, a dark car appeared out of nowhere and rammed his truck from behind. He cursed and pulled over. Out of the night, arms snatched him from the cab and all I could see was shadowy figures disappearing in the black hole that swallowed them up. I jumped from the truck and headed down the ditch, doing a little name calling myself. Bodies pushed pass me, knocking me down as they rushed by and up the incline to their waiting car. My first impulse was to run after them, but tires squealed, dust billowed and the car sped away.

I whirled and called Mike. Following his moan, I stumbled through the low brush and saw him, knees drawn up, face in the sand, the moonlight glistening white on his back. "Mike!" I shouted, tugging at his shoulders. My hands slipped, he felt wet and sticky, like... "Mike, talk to me!" His head was wet but everything was black and white so I couldn't tell whether it was blood.

"I'm okay, Rhea." He pushed himself up, grunted and held his side, but got to his feet, wiping at his face. "Just give me a minute."

"I'm going for help, Mike. Stay still."

He grabbed my hand and said, "No. Help—just help me to the truck, but when I tugged on his arm, it slipped through my fingers. Finally, I got him in the truck and when I slid behind the wheel, for the first time I noticed an acrid stench encircling us. "I don't think I'm hurt, Rhea. There's just... I don't know what it is, but it stinks."

We topped the last step of his deck and when I turned on the lights, I saw slimy, yellow globs in his hair and on the top half of his body. "What is this?" Pushing him into the bathroom, I snatched a towel, wet it and started wiping his face. "Mike, you need a shower. Let me help you get undressed."

"Yeah," he murmured. He'd been so quiet, I wondered what he was thinking and glanced at his dazed, but scowling face. "I'll undress in there. It's rotten—eggs, fish—I don't know..."

"Are you okay?"

"Yes."

When he entered the living room, bruises were already showing up on his face and there were scratches on his arms. I made him sit down, swabbed his cuts with mercurochrome, and begged him to let me call the police. He assured me it wouldn't do any good, that he'd tried that before. "If you won't do that, at least let's go to an Emergency Room and be sure you're okay." He shook his head, and I could almost feel the pent-up rage. While we put his clothes in the washing machine and cleaned the bathroom, he opened up when I kept insisting he explain what he meant by "before." Stunned, I listened while he cited the sequence of unreal events: the dead cat stuffed in his mailbox, the skunk incident, garbage at his door, tires slashed, eggs on his truck, and now this. The story would have made a good script for a horror show. "Who would do this malicious stuff to you?"

"I wish I knew."

"There's a theme here. We just need to sort it all…"

"Yeah. Someone wants me to leave." He pulled out the letters—ten times what he'd showed me before—and spread them over the table. Bewildered, I read the cut up words, covering page after page. "YOU'RE DOOMED!" "HELL CALLS YOU!" and tonight they'd pinned one to his shirt, "THE FIRE YOU FEEL IN YOUR BELLY IS THE EVIL IN YOUR SOUL."

I stared at this person I'd seen splint a gull's wing, patiently curry sand-spurs from Delilah's coat and play with Charlotte's children, and declared, "You couldn't kill a field mouse."

He took my hand. "Rhea, I strafed bridges, troops, villages… We bombed everything that moved."

"You had to!" I shouted. "You said yourself…"

Brightening, he whispered, "That's it! Anti-war activists! The last message said, 'Leave Warmonger!'"

"Maybe, but Mike, your ordeal in the POW camp far outweighs your obeying orders. Have you showed these notes to the police?" He sighed, shook his head and I saw the heavy-lidded gaze; the muscle relaxers I'd given him were working. "What about the dead animals and…"

"There's nothing they can do. I don't have names or proof."

"Dead animals and letters aren't proof?" I cried. "I know, they want hard facts. We'll figure it out. Who'd want you to leave? Think, Mike!"

"Trey's the only one who'd want me out of the way." He lifted his swollen face. His eyes were too bright, he looked pale, and I started to ask him again if he felt okay when he said, "There's one other person I've considered, Rhea. Lowell."

After going over and over the particulars, we still came up with insubstantial proof, agreeing Lowell's motives and nature just weren't strong enough to go to such lengths. Tactfully, I hinted at family members which he adamantly rejected, but in the end we agreed not to totally reject anyone.

It was getting late, and he seemed so exhausted, I left, inviting him to my place for a hot breakfast for which he thanked me, reminding me he'd be up and gone before dawn. Weary myself, I trudged across the sand, turning it all over in my mind and was afraid for him.

Two days later, Natalie called around mid-morning. She sounded worried, saying Mike didn't show up for his and Randy's charter. She'd called, but he didn't answer. She asked me to look outside and see if his truck was there, adding, "It's just not like him. Even Randy's concerned," renewing my fear and causing a ripple of uneasiness between my shoulder blades.

His truck sat in its usual spot. I rushed to the telephone and told Natalie, promising to go over, have a look and call her back.

When I tried his sliding door, I found it unlocked, and stepped inside. The first thing I noticed was the air; it hung thick and humid despite the thump, thump of the overhead fan. Trying to sort through the sudden apprehension I sensed in the familiar room, I realized groans were coming from his bedroom.

Intermittently shivering and whimpering, Mike lay amid

twisted sheets, and when I touched his shoulder, I jerked my hand away from the fierce heat. I picked up a bottle on his bedside table. Quinine! Frantically, I called Natalie, and she confirmed he'd had bouts of malaria before, saying she'd call his doctor. In a few short minutes, Natalie called back saying Dr. Seymour would be right over.

The doctor arrived, poked Mike's stomach, took his temperature and checked his blood pressure. He instructed me to fetch a spoon and poured out some of the medicine. He raised Mike's head, forced the clear liquid between his lips and rubbed his throat. Mike grimaced. The doctor told me to repeat the dose in four hours with two aspirin, and to call him an hour afterwards.

After he left, I reported in to Natalie offering to stay with Mike until his fever broke. Then I went into the living room and flipped through a *Field & Stream*, but couldn't concentrate. Unable to ignore Mike's moaning and thrashing, I returned to his bedroom, sat beside him and wiped his face with a wet cloth. Half an hour later, I checked his temperature. It was lower, and he finally slept peacefully. I fell asleep, but sometime during the night, he woke me yelling and scrambling from the bed. He ended up in the corner on the floor, cowering and shaking. I touched his forehead. Fever again! Battling his arms, I managed to get another dose of the quinine and aspirin down, then held his trembling body tightly. I wanted to cry when he sobbed, "Hold me, Mandy. I'm so cold." What seemed hours later, I got him back into bed and he rested quietly. Wrapped in his robe, I curled up beside him and tried to sleep, waking every time he moved or mumbled, repeating the medicine whenever I could and wiping his hot face, arms and legs with alcohol. The sun was high when he woke and asked why I was there.

Seven

Damn this rain! Randy called earlier with news I'd already figured out. You really need avid fishers to go out in this cold slop, and that wasn't the case with today's anglers. Tomorrow, I bet it'll clear up, but it's Saturday, and we don't have a customer. Maybe today's folks will stay over and want to try again, not that Randy seems to need the money. You would think with as much rain as we've had these last weeks and with nearly as many canceled charters, he'd feel a little nervous. Instead, he said he and Diane were going to Biloxi to do some shopping. So why am I worried? It's not like I need the money either. The lump the Air Force paid me is invested in Savings Bonds, and I've saved almost half of what I've made working with Randy, so I'm set. It's just that I get so bored.

I wish Rhea was home. She's been gone for days—the story of my life—but sometimes I think I feel her presence. I could build a fire and read, or watch television, or go into town for supplies, or clean this dive. All these "ought to's" try to edge in, but I'd rather think of her, and shake them off. Ever since we met, she's been my best friend, but lately, she's passed the ultimate loyalty test, placing her on the highest pedestal I can find—and still keeping her within reach. She helped me clean up that vile mess after that last, and worst attack and then nursed me through a bout of malaria. After I regrouped my wits, I asked her why she didn't call Natalie or Mom to come, but my heart went lickety-split when she said she wanted to take care of me.

God, I miss her! I swore I'd never care for anyone like this again, and here I am, right in the middle of love. But she's got a life, too, a fact I need to keep reminding myself. And from all indications, I'm not sure I'm going to play a major role in it.

Maybe if I could concentrate and clear up what's causing my other headaches—namely the threats—the pieces of the whole puzzle would fall into place. Might as well start by trying to sort through this more visible chaos: my house. I need to do some serious cleaning. Yuck! Oh, well, I'll slap some jive music on the old player and dive in. Then I do need to go to town. Better make a list: dog food, groceries, and mustn't forget the hardware store for a new hammer handle.

What's put me in this gloomy mood? The weather? Rhea's absence? Even Delilah moans and groans each time she relocates. She's restless, too. Of course she doesn't like the vacuum's noise any more than I like wrestling with it. And letting Randy and Diane talk me into taking Diane's friend, Janie, to the movies last night, then letting Janie talk me into seeing *The Bridge on the River Kwai*, made me feel like something low and spineless. Why do I do that shitty stuff, see a story about British POW's, for chrissake!

Don't sit down again, you slouch! But I'm already reeling under the bulky weight of worthlessness. If I sit down with a book—Ha! That's a joke! You've been sitting all day! What? Oh, yeah, don't remind me. What's that old saying, "Absence makes the heart grow fonder?" It's working one-sided, Conscience, old buddy. Rhea doesn't know I'm alive. There's a wall I can almost feel growing between us. So what are you doing about it? Listen, she's in New York, you know. Taking a class—like she needs it—getting something done—And you, what are you doing? Lemme alone! For the moment, I'm just gonna grovel. But all I really want is to walk the beach with her, hold her hand and listen to her talk. That's a lie! Boy, you're playing rough today. Okay. I want more—I want her here and close. Am I asking too much? It doesn't count until you make a move. Besides, if she's gone all the time anyway—Cut it out!

Delilah's worried. She hasn't moved, but her eyes follow me around. She can read my mind, too. Jesus, I must be an open book! Now she's ambled over, nudging my limp hand, whined and plopped down at my feet. "It's okay, girl. If I go, you can come, too, even though sometimes I wonder if she loves you more than me!" What a joker you are! Who said anything about her loving you? I'm not listening to you, do you hear? Get lost!

Right now, I might as well tackle these dirty clothes and dishes; I'd rather let it all slide but it isn't going anywhere. This house, not unlike my existence, is one grand mess.

Sometimes, like the night the car pulled us over, I believe my life's in jeopardy. Hell's bells, Rhea could have been hurt! She's in danger simply by associating with me! I've got to figure this mystery out and put a stop to this antagonizing. Then, when she gets back, tell her the whole truth and see if

I can't convince her we belong together. What if she has no intention of returning? She hasn't called or written. You dunce, she never has before either. You've never asked her to and before you do you'd better be prepared to let your intentions—lay all the cards on the table, so to speak—be known. You realize, of course, if you two were to—What? Do you want to marry her? Yes! Well, you'll be the one sitting home alone night after night. To expect her to change her lifestyle would totally destroy any love she feels for you. Are you willing to live waiting for her next return? Yes! Then I suggest you get on with it. You're right! As soon as she gets home, I'm going to tell her!

Outside, a mourning dove tries to lull me into melancholia. Well, I'm already there, bird. Don't need your help, but I'd sure like to know if she meant what she said a few nights ago. Now what are you trying to read into friendly overtures? Anyone who cared a whit about someone would say the same any day of the week! Boy, you've sure improved my mood! Go away! The blasted rain pounding the roof is dreary enough without you adding your two cents worth. Last night, it was even worst sitting in that movie with Janie and all those strangers. When I was a kid, I remember having to finish some chores I'd put off, rushing to the ball field where all my friends were waiting, but they had been called home to supper—that's the kind of loneliness I felt in the hulking auditorium, not to mention the eerie lights flickering on zombie spectators.

Holy smokes! I almost forgot! I'd promised Sonny and Shallie a picnic at Fort Chinquefield tomorrow. Kids don't understand about rain and love. Better phone Charlotte and warn her right now, 'cause if I wait and have to cancel because I've gotta work, they'll drive her batty, and she'll probably think of some new names for me.

Last week when I told Shallie and Sonny about the colony, I hoped Rhea would be back and could go with us.

Just like them, I knew she'd love the story about the settlement's menfolks going out to hunt for food. The kids' eyes nearly popped out when I told them about the Creek Indians slipping into the village, massacring the women and children as they did their laundry in the stream's clear water, leaving only two survivors. Are they too young to tell these scary stories to? Evidently not. They hadn't batted an eye, just begged to go there!

Besides, I'd given them a good laugh when I told them Grandfather Kipling's story about Ronnie Skelton, the town's tough. Just like he'd told me years ago, I described the split log benches in the school room, and I could almost see the creative wheels churning when I told them about Ronnie and his buddies putting straight pins in the cracks—point up, of course. The highlight was when I said, "Picture this, kids. The girls came in and sat down, immediately springing into the air, screaming at the top of their lungs." They giggled when I added, "Huge tears rolled down those girls' cheeks," and their eyes grew big as saucers when I told them about the teacher sending the boys out to pick their own switches. I had their undivided attention when I took one of my kite sticks and illustrated how, on their way back to the school house, the boys used their pocket knives to ring the tender twigs. They clapped when I described the teacher's face after laying those limp sticks across the imps' flesh, and I decided I'd better make up some punishment quick before they got the wrong idea. But even after I told them the boys stood in the corner for hours, they sniggered, and I remembered I'd rolled in a fit of laughter the first time I'd heard this story, too. Charlotte would recognize the tale, and she'd sure come after me if her two thought up some way to put it to use, so I'd tried to play it down with another story but, those imps keep after me for more details.

Getting nothing done for being caught up in the wistful

grip of memories, I continued to sentimentalize over Grandad's words. He'd ramble on about how when he was a boy the summers were so hot and dry the pines would raise their arms heavenward, begging for rain, dusty red roads would choke you just for walking down them, and that once the sun's heat fused the riverbank's limestone, turning it into white marble. We'd sit out at twilight and he'd speak of yellow days and curse the movie houses and the radio—"GD contraptions—warping your tender mind!" he promised, while I caught lightning bugs, clapping them into a glass jar. That same night, holding me spellbound, he told about catching an alligator gar that pulled his skiff from the mouth of Biloxi Bay, past the old lighthouse, almost to the Gulf's barrier islands. Then he informed me that the fireflies I'd caught were gentlemen courting ladies and that's how glowworms came to be. For a minute, I almost let them go, but my regrets, short-lived those days, died and I sneaked the bottle into bed with me to watch their flickering lights under the cover, never giving courtship or reproduction another thought.

Grandad used to talk about pink-rimmed horizons at sunset, too, and new stars and finding artesian wells. Remembering some of these yarns in the camp, it dawned on me my grandfather had been quite a storyteller. Someday soon I'll tell Rhea his tales, but with my luck, she'd wander back into the past forever, in love with Grandad! Well, anyway, I've managed to wade through a few chores while sojourning down memory lane.

Finally, the rain slacked. Randy couldn't reschedule the anglers, so Sonny, Shallie and I tramped through the wet woods to the fort's falling down remains. We sat on the creek's bank and ate the lunch I packed, with a lot of help from Ma and Pop Steelman and their grocery store, while I told them all the gory, passed-along details essential to the historic site's fascination. They devoured every word and morsel like youngsters do, and with full tummies, wanted to look for blood-soaked arrowheads and bones. When I dropped them off, they hardly noticed I'd left, they were so busy telling their mother about the carnage. Charlotte's really gonna love me now!

Maybe it's the unusually warm March day feeding my nostalgia, but when I drove under the rusty railroad trestle just south of Gossport and saw a patch of buttercups waving along the roadside, I missed Grandad again and thought of how the first of every summer he'd trick me into a sniff, dusting my nose yellow.

Buttercups and a pale blue sky, but I'm getting off the track. Two nights ago, a new idea took root. Natalie invited me to dinner and during the meal she'd said, "Gramma's house..." but stopped, gazing at me bizarrely, then continued, "Gramma's house needs lots of work. I don't think Char and Julian can afford the repairs." Somehow I didn't believe that's what she'd intended to say especially since we'd been talking about me taking Shallie and Sonny to the fort and Grandad's stories. Suddenly, exploding back in time, I could hear Gramma saying, "This house will be yours someday!" That, plus Charlotte's baseless words a few weeks before, "You always were the pet," made me suspicious, and so today, I'm out playing gumshoe.

Squinting at its brilliance, I glanced up at the Court House's white dome and suspected a fresh coat of paint. On the clock tower, black Roman numerals stood out like a game's playing pieces, and facing north, south, east and west, some titan's mislaid swords pointed to four-twenty. Drats! Everyone knew the doors were locked at noon on Saturday's even though the red and white banner above the double oak doors invited, "Visit Our Museum!"

I turned west onto Mount Pleasant Avenue and braked. There, around back, an open door leading into a cavernous hallway waited somberly. I parked, leaped up the worn, granite steps and stepped inside, plunging into an imposing, cool past. Tangy odors reminiscent of pencil sharpener shavings and rotting newspapers demanded reverence as I walked across solid, oiled floors. Down the wide hallway I passed wooden doors with bumpy glass inserts lettered with names like "Tax Collector," "Judge Aycock" and "Records," where I stopped. Inside, as familiar with the paper-stuffed files as her own reflection, I knew ancient Mrs. Hopkins, her silvery hair slicked back into a tight wad, could put her bony hands on deeds, wills, and Lord knows what else.

Gripping the slick wood counter with sweaty hands, I cleared my throat. Mrs. Hopkins whirled. Her starched plaid dress crackled, and I smiled weakly at a vaguely familiar scowl.

Life's a big mistake, I thought, walking outside and standing in the sunshine, my ears ringing with contradictions. We're born, taught what's right and wrong in the eyes of our preappointed clan and set free. But what holds a family together? Compassion and patience—virtues my parents taught—are handy from time to time, but deserted me when I heard about Mandy's anguish. Followed by a scientifically induced cure, she'd divorced me and married my best friend, Trey, and then.... The all too familiar facts left me traumatized and illogical.

For long years I had loved Mandy unfalteringly. At times, her essence alone kept me clearheaded and directed. Although at first I'd thought my parents inhuman when they'd held she'd served her purpose, evidenced by my survival, later, in calmer moments, I accepted their explanation. Even when I heard Gramma and Grandad died while I lay in a cell somewhere in North Korea, I'd wondered why the blows didn't get easier since I'd become perpetually braced for these eroding announcements. But months passed, and I came to understand living carried its rewards along with its sacrifices and through all this I decided if we had a choice, we shouldn't try to stand alone facing throat-constricting fear or death's cruel snap. What does it take these days to feel thankful, to forgive, to see beauty and to laugh? Basically, I still kept my opinions submerged, a good example: loving Rhea. However, I believe that with the passage of time, judgment's narrow edge grows wider and stronger, heaving us from darkness to light, and finally into revelation, flavored with a dash of humor, much like the ecstasy of love.

No more backward glances, I swore, but all these beliefs scared me. That and too much knowledge, I concluded when Mrs. Hopkins' double, her spinster daughter, handed me a bombshell from the grave: a copy of Gramma's will.

Shallie's shrill little girl laughter whirled down the hall, through the screen and past my face like the wind tinkling the glass Japanese wind chimes on the porch. I imagined her teasing Sonny, him whining, later squalling. Charlotte used to do the same to me. "Shallie, stop pestering Sonny!" my sister yelled. "And pick up those blocks before he hurts himself." Mother's words verbatim. An outsider looking in on reality, flung from the past to the present, I grinned and knocked on the sagging screen door.

When Charlotte continued barking, my fingers coiled around the worn knob and I experienced a new intimacy with the old house's nails and boards when I pulled the door open. "Charlotte?" I hollered. "Hey, Char, it's me, Mike."

Her head popped from the kitchen. Both youngsters pushed past her, heading my way. She wiped her hands roughly on her apron, stepped into the hall and a menacing breeze preceded her scowl. Still mad, no doubt about it. And I may never know the whole reason, but I'm above her anger now, and ready to let the wound heal.

Shallie yelled, "Uncle Mike!" and ran toward me. At least someone's glad to see me! Sonny plugged his mouth with his thumb and wrapped his other arm about his mother's leg. Then he let go, wobbled, took a step and sat down hard on the wood floor.

"Look at you! Char, when did he start walking?" I snatched Shallie up and started toward my sister and the baby.

"Yesterday," she said hotly, wheeling and vanishing into the kitchen.

If words could seal a passage, hers were iron and for an instant, I froze. I stepped to the door and spoke to her riveted back. "God Almighty, I wish you'd tell me why you're so angry at me. Don't I deserve to know?"

She dipped to gather Sonny, slung him to her hip and turned to the sink. "Do you want some coffee? And please, don't curse in front of the children."

"Charlotte, please. We need to talk."

"What's curse, Uncle Mike?"

"Saying bad words, Shallie. I said 'God' and you shouldn't say that unless you're talking to Him."

One small arm held my neck, a pudgy hand pushed my face toward hers and she asked, "You were talking to him, weren't you?" I smiled at the clouded, blue eyes even with mine. "Weren't you?"

"Sort of, baby."

"Mike!"

When I looked at Charlotte's face, I felt tired, but determined. Her nose flared, and her lips were pale and tense. I set Shallie on the floor and the disappointed four-year-old looked up at me. "Let me just get a hug from Sonny, baby, and then, I need to talk to your mommy. Afterwards, if Mommy doesn't mind, I'll take you both for a walk on the beach. Okay? In the meantime, why don't you play with Son? Build him a house or a car with those pretty blocks."

"I don't have any wheels. You can't make a car without wheels."

"You're exactly right. A house will be just fine." I straightened and picked up the cup Charlotte pushed across the table toward me and sniffed. Like Gramma, she always could make good coffee. And on the stove's burner, sat the friendly blue and gray metal pot, or an exact replica. Inside, a cloth bag on a circle of wire would be filled with coffee. I took a sip. There was no doubt she'd inherited Gramma's secret too. "Ummm. That itsy-bitsy pinch of salt, right?" Instantly overcome with grief, I realized Gramma never showed me how big an "itsy-bitsy pinch" was, but Char knew. "This tastes just like Gramma's," I murmured, watching Charlotte's hard face.

She turned and started running water at the sink, giving me her silent treatment. Reflecting on all the wasted years, I begged, "Why won't you talk to me? If I've done something wrong, I'm sorry, but how can I ever make amends if I don't know what it is?" Silence. "Char, I know about Gramma's will and the house."

That got her attention. First, she looked at me over her shoulder, then she turned and faced me, bracing against the counter. "So now I guess you want us to move out. Is that why you're here?"

"Is that what you think? Has worrying I'd find out and evict you been the problem? I almost wish that's all it is, Char. No. As far as I'm concerned, the house is yours. Do you understand? I want you, Julian and the kids to have the house. We'll fix up a bill of sale for a dollar; however you want to handle it is okay, let's just make it legal.

"What bothers me is, why couldn't you come to me? Why this stony silence all these months? Didn't you think we could sit down and talk about it like—adults?" Trancelike, she stared at me. Unsure whether I'd reached her or not, I took a deep breath and forged ahead. "There's more to this, isn't there?"

She shook her head.

"You're lying."

Her brown eyes, dull with hate, bored holes in me through which I felt my courage oozing out, but she parted her lips just slightly. This is it! She's going to burst open and let a million pent-up words fly in my direction, but that's good!

"You can't make it right! You think you can just waltz back into our lives and everything's okay? Take your house, but the money's gone. Things were going pretty good until…"

Oh, God, no! Not her! Surely she's not the one. "Until I came back, right? Say it, Charlotte."

She trembled. Her lips drew up into a wrinkled, white slit, and for a moment I thought I saw a tear.

"Come on, Char. For over six months we've been walking on eggshells around each other. I'm ready to be your friend and your brother, but first, you're going to have to let me. Spill your guts, scream, curse, whatever it takes, just be truthful."

"Julian says—Anyway, we deserve the house. You've got no family. The money—After you'd been gone long enough, we had you declared legally dead. Randy, Nat and I divided your share. Our's is gone. Julian had run up some debts."

"None of this interests me, Char. The money, the house. It's not worth losing you and your kids or Julian. What's done is done. We can't change it anymore than we can bring back Gramma and Grandad. Are you sure that's all? Do you need to go back further, like when we were kids?

"That's why Julian says we deserve everything we got. You always got the best of everything. First you were Mom and Dad's pet; then Gramma—"

"Wait. When did all this start?"

She sobbed, "I wanted that damned rifle so bad."

"I thought so. I'm sorry, Char, but so did I, and at ten—I don't really have an excuse, all I can say is, in my little boy's mind, I felt the same way you and Julian did about the house, I guess. When I shot that moccasin, and Dad said I deserved that rifle, I wanted to believe him.

"In the camp I had lots of time to think. You—all my family for that matter—were on my mind constantly. I wanted to get back to you almost as bad as I did to Mandy. You and I...We needed another chance, I prayed we'd get it, and we did. I guess every child imagines they're a stepchild sometimes. It wasn't anything Mom and Dad did. It was the resentment I sensed... Did you know there were a few years I was so afraid of you—You were, and still are, so pretty, but you were strong, too. Remember the time you pushed me down and I thought my brains were spilling out? Talk about scared I'd make you mad again!" All at once, I knew I wasn't getting through. Charlotte's eyes glazed over after that first outburst and she sat across the table, her hands clasped and she guarded her hate as vigorously as she did her love. "What are you feeling, Charlotte?"

"Disgust!" she spat. "I'm sitting here listening to you babble about second chances, letting bygones be bygones, and wanting to call you an adulterer. You forget Mandy and I were best friends before she met you! I introduced you two at that party, remember? At least Mandy behaved herself appropriately in your absence."

The gist of her words baffled me. Clearly, there were some obscure details or events I knew nothing about, or that she misinterpreted. Stupefied, and seeing the determined expression on my sister's face, I realized I might never win her over and in all probability, battled with disturbed hatred.

"Well, what do you think Mandy's going to feel when she finds out you've got—" She dashed to the back door and stared out.

"Go ahead, Charlotte," I whispered, lost and a little dazed. "What have I got?"

"Illegitimate children," she hissed.

Her words slammed like a battering ram into my chest. Starved for air, I gasped, "What are you talking about?"

"You said it—" she growled. "You told that artist neighbor of yours you were going back to Korea to get two children." She'd placed both hands on the table and thrust her face close to mine. "There aren't many ways that can be taken."

"Char—"

"Yes, tell me. I'm most anxious to hear about your long, lonely years in the POW camp. Did they provide concubines?" My mind raced around looking for answers. Rhea hadn't screwed up the facts this bad. Somewhere between Natalie and Charlotte, and who knows, maybe Randy, too, somebody, or all of them, took liberties with their translation. Shades of the whisper game, and I'd passed my patience threshold. "Visualize this, Charlotte. Two innocent children, just a little older than Shallie and Sonny had their heads lobbed off because their family helped me. Their small bodies just hung, suspended for what seemed like forever, blood gushing—"

"Shallie, take Sonny upstairs!"

Fighting for control, I closed my eyes and pressed my hands against my temples. "To adopt orphans, Char," I mumbled, pushing my chair back. "I was going to adopt—" Charlotte's bearing reeked doubt, and out of my peripheral vision, I saw Shallie watching me, her little girl eyes filled with confusion. "You don't honestly believe…" but my sister's steely look told me she did. I stumbled to the back door, out and down the steps.

"Uncle Mike, you promised—"

"We'll go another time, baby."

Shallie cried, "Uncle Mike!" over and over, but I couldn't look back. I ran down the beach until my heart pumped in my ears and my lungs hurt. *You're losing it,* buddy. Maybe the letters were right! Maybe you shouldn't have come back.

Someone knocked at the door, but I was fast on the way to falling-down drunk and busy allowing some pot Tess left on her last visit to manipulate my hands and legs, so moving was next to impossible, if I'd wanted to—but I didn't. Sharper and sharper, the rapping continued, something metallic clinking against glass. Chuckling, I slid to the sofa's seat, hoping when I disappeared from view, whoever was knocking would leave. I shut my eyes. My body floated and I found the euphoric sensation pleasing, the noise less troublesome. A voice called. Who gives a shit! For all I care, they can scream their head's off! I snickered cruelly. Seems I'm hung up on heads falling off. I laughed, didn't want to talk, much less listen to sermonizing. The cryptic music playing in my head would do just fine, could go on forever as far as I was concerned. Maybe I could sleep for a year or two in this snugness and wake up in... Let's see. Where would I like to go?

Eight

"It's Sunday—I think."

Natalie shook her head, and I didn't know if I'd passed her sobriety and mental agility test or not. One thing I did know, I'd over-done my binge this time. My head feels like it got caught in the cross-fire of two boxers slugging it out for the Welterweight Championship. I'm sitting here trying to hold its pieces together—it must be in at least a dozen—and my kid sister's pouring me another cup of old motor oil she calls coffee. Now she's pleading with me to go back to Charlotte's—like I need some more abuse—because Charlotte's sorry. Big deal, Nat! I wanted to shout but my mouth was packed with cotton. Have you been in my funny weeds? No. Better not say that either, besides I think I finished it off. Furthermore, Char can come to me if she's so sorry!

I think I've heard this already, too, but Nat's telling me she had no idea Charlotte interpreted the story about me going to Korea to adopt two children the way she did. She says Char's syrupy, "How sweet," rang sincerely enough to her. It turns out the big problem was, Nat didn't finish the story thinking Char knew it already, especially when she'd made that comment. Anyway, Charlotte knows the whole truth now and she's sorry. "Good! Yes, Natalie, I think I've got all that straight." Now I just wish she would go home and let me practice my, Rhea, I love you's! Thank God, Rhea's coming home tomorrow, because I've had it up to my eyeballs with my family.

Now Nat's talking to Randy on the phone. She's telling him I'm not feeling too well when I snatched the receiver and listened. "Goddamnit! He'd better get well in a hurry! We've got big-shot anglers who want to take some fucking big business buddies out for fucking grouper!"

"That's no way to talk to your sister, Ran. Cool down, fella! I'll be there."

"Mike, damnit! We've got to go out at least thirty miles—"

"I know. Just tell me what time. I'll be there."

"Have your butt here—and sober, Goddamnit—at four."

"Okay."

"Will you be there?"

"Is the equator still in the same place, little brother?" I knew that would get his goat. He slammed the receiver down, I groaned and lay back on the sofa. Terrific! He's right though. Grouper means way out, fishing on the bottom, and these guys better be as strong as their money. We'll fish the reef, the wrecked plane—all two hundred feet or more below the surface. These baby's like to hide in holes and when they hit the bait, Randy's gotta move the boat forward in a hurry, and the anglers must wind fast, take up any slack and keep the line tight. The deep sea rods are heavy, you've got to be in good shape, so guess who's gonna have to work their butt off hauling in whose forty pound, plus or minus an ounce or two, grouper?

How about, Rhea, I think I loved you from the first moment I saw you? Great! That ought to get a laugh. She and I both know at that point of my life, I hated all women's guts!

All right, let's work on the next problem. When am I going to tell her all this stuff? Tomorrow night's her big exhibit. Am I going to do it during or after? Listen, Rhea, I love you. I want to marry you, today, if possible. Okay? What if she laughs? Holy cow! What if she doesn't!

The charter was every bit as bad as I expected, but Randy, bless his soul, got us in before the rental store closed. By the time I drove across the bay, picked up my tux, drove home, showered and dressed, my arrival should be just about right, the last hour of her show. Nat and Max will be there, but so will Lowell. I'd sworn Nat to secrecy, but there wasn't much I could do about Lowell. And he'd take Rhea home, so when— Take it easy! I'll just ask to take her home. If she says no, maybe I'll wait up for her. It'll happen! I'm ready. I know this is right. It'll happen, damnit!

I looked around the crowded, smoke-filled room. A blonde in see-through black smiled and fluttered her lush eyelashes when I passed. A sociable bartender chatted about the thirsty crowd, fixed me a bourbon and water and I edged toward Rhea's paintings, looking for her.

Three musicians huddled in a corner. One banged a piano, one blew into a trumpet and the other into a sax. The music was brassy and thought-shattering. They probably called it improvised jazz, but it sounded more like unrehearsed bedlam to my ears. Too damned loud, Rhea. What's your ass of an agent thinking about? But Lowell, in the expected frilly-fronted monkey-suit, smiled, all teeth and no heart. The way he squints you can't tell there's emptiness behind his eyes, and he nods all the time, like one of those yellow and red wooden birds I saw in a store window, dipping its beak into a glass of water. Funny, he actually looks nervous. The music's enough to make anyone nervous—it's bouncing off the walls, stunning my eardrums.

What's going on in that little alcove? Bold black letters—"A E L." Curious. I moved closer and saw an "H," further left, "C" and—Naw, it can't be! I stood in the opening, and there above four paintings, in bold black, I read, "THE COLORS OF MICHAEL." But when I moved into the cordoned room, I blinked. What the hell!

The first canvas was a view from inside a room. Although my eyes were drawn outside, to the beach and bright blue water, I stared at the jumbled scene created by broad, short dabs from a heavily loaded brush—her favorite way to paint—complete with spilled flowers, a toppled table, and me—no doubt about it—on the floor, glowering and thin, like I was in those days—with long hair, a beard, and even the end of a crutch sticking from beneath my rear. Our first meeting! Red predominated; she had gotten mad.

Dazed, I moved to the right, wondering why I hadn't seen these. Of course, I don't spend that much time over there, but several times a week I drop by to see how she's doing.

In the next canvas—a profile of me—I'm sitting on the beach at sunset staring out at sea, one arm balanced limply over a propped-up knee, a few strands of hair lifted high in the breeze. The colors are soft blues and purple. Not our brilliant sunsets, but I remember feeling this coolness, seeing these exact colors without seeing them at all.

Like turning the pages in a book, I move to the third

painting and laugh. I remember this! Delilah's eyes pleading with me after I'd thrown a piece of driftwood into the surf—Spaniels are supposed to like water! I'd cajoled her, she'd whined, running back and forth along the shore until in I go, up to my waist, grab the stick and call her. Finally, wanting to make me happy, get a pat on head or a treat when we got back to the house, she'd plunged in. Of course, all this wasn't on the canvas, just me wading, holding the stick, eyes slits to the sun, laughing, and Delilah making that first leap into space, braced for the shock of the cold water. But Rhea caught the glistening spray on my face, arms and chest, dripping from my hair as though the wave just slapped my back, spewing all around Delilah's freckled beige body, feathers flying in the wind, ears out like Dumbo making that headlong, spiralling glide from the ladder into a bucket of water. Perfect! What a cartoon! And she'd captured it in a frozen frame of sand-colored, shaded and tinted, action.

Beginning to feel self-conscious, I glanced around. Other people were nearby, drinks in hands, pretending to look at the paintings, but more concerned with what they were saying and how they looked. Anyhow, Rhea's deft technique skirts true identity—at least to my inept judgment—and only the two of us could possibly know about these moments. I shrugged and moved on.

This one's late evening; rosy shadows lit with a hint of the day's last light, holding onto the horizon like Rhea's holding my hand, her ghostly white sundress billowing in the wind. The day returned like I'd been transported back into time. It was the same day I'd met with Mandy. There was no way in the world she could have known, but it felt like she did. Aimlessly, I stumbled, dragging a stick in the sand when Rhea ran up behind me. She'd slipped her hand in mine, saw my tears but didn't say a word. Her touch dismissed tension, purifying my body like baptism. Heathen that I'd been then,

I'd wanted her so fiercely I couldn't even say hello. Calmly, she'd taken the stick, along with my sadness, and dragged it for me. We'd walked and walked until dark. There had been no moon. In the distance, car lights dotted and dashed through the bay bridge's superstructure. But in a flash, I recalled the low tide's soft slapping around pier pilings, our steps squeaking on the packed sand and popping in my ears like a frenzied bird throwing itself against a reflective windowpane. All the time, Rhea's conversation touched on one light-hearted subject after another: the weather's increasing turbulence; Adlai Stevenson's witty book she'd just finished, making me promise to borrow it from her; how sorry she was that I'd missed seeing Mary Martin fly through "Peter Pan"—with the help of wires; the Bridey Murphy revelation—but promised to make me a Reincarnation Cocktail; and the chlorophyll craze and the scientist saying it didn't help the goats. She had me laughing so hard I sat down on the cold sand, fighting the urge to pull her down and make love to her right then and there.

But if all this means what I think...

Bashfully, I shook my head and looked around. How long had I been standing there? No suspicious stares met mine, so I tried to compose myself before going to look for her.

I walked back into the main room and looked around. There she was, by the canapé table. She sees me. Her eyebrows lift, and her wide eyes ask What do you think? I smiled and nodded. She sets her glass down and heads my way—get ready—but suddenly, Lowell steps out of nowhere, his nose not four inches from mine.

Low and ominous like the distant tramp of an approaching army, his voice rolls, "You think I don't know what's going on? Pretty sneaky son-of-a-bitch thing to do. Rhea's got talent. Can you help her? Can you arrange her shows? You don't know crap about this business." I'm not going to let him make me mad! "All you know is smelly fish, drinking beer with the locals and wallowing in self-pity because you got left behind in some frigging war you probably didn't even believe in!"

"Lowell!" Rhea hissed fiercely at his elbow.

"Listen to me, my dear," he pleaded sweetly, his tone reversing to a insidious whine. "Your guests believe you're making a statement, and we'll just play it up like this is a new style you're trying out on them." He stopped, his eyes skimming the crowd. "Smell the money. Tonight they'll buy!"

I stepped up. "Rhea, I need to talk to—"

With a stupid grin plastered on his face, Lowell tried to push me aside. I planted my feet and held my ground.

"Rhea, we can fix this. Step aside, buddy." Again, Lowell tried to wedge himself between me and Rhea. "Rhea, if you have any control over this—Look, I'll forget your not letting me in on this spectacle, but do you want to destroy everything we've worked for? Everyone's whispering!"

Rhea stiffened. "I don't care what anyone thinks. This is my show, something I wanted to do and I didn't need to consult—"

"Because you knew I'd nix the idea!"

On the verge of exploding, I put my hand on Lowell's chest and pushed him back a step or two. "Excuse me, Lowell. Get out of her face. Regardless of what you think—"

"Listen, buddy—"

"Mike, let's go. I'm just not in the mood to listen to his ravings." She reached for my arm, but Lowell grabbed her wrist and my hackles rose. I grabbed his wrist and ordered, "Let—her—go."

People turned to watch. In the second or two that followed, the whole room fell silent. Rhea looked around nervously and smiled, but the three of us were locked in a standoff: Lowell's hand on her wrist, mine on his. "Rhea, there are influential people here," he hissed. "Buying clients. Tell—him—to—back off." I wanted to laugh. Beads of sweat stood on his upper lip and across his brow, but thin, ebbing battle squeaked from his mouth. "This could ruin your career."

"Let her go, Lowell, and step aside or I'll have to hit you."

"Shut up, you bourgeois beach bum!" Lowell snapped. "Make him let go or this is it, Rhea! I've had enough of his interfering, his influence—Look how ordinary your work's become." He started to wave his free hand at the four paintings and I hit his chin with all my might. He foundered backwards, dragging Rhea, crashing into the food-laden, flower-bedecked table, and the whole smear folded like a domino row, lapping up several bystanders in the wave.

Apologizing, I helped Rhea up, found a napkin in the pile of olives, stuffed celery, crackers and cheese and brushed drops of champagne from her chin and nose. Her dark eyes darted around, got shiny and I knew she was about to cry. "Here, let me help you—" Nostrils flaring, she pushed me aside and sprang upright, snatched a bottle of champagne from the bar, and swung around to the ogling, stupefied onlookers. "Party's over, folks," she shouted. "Go home!" She turned to me, took my hand and dragged me from the room.

Outside, she shivered. I took off my jacket and draped it over her shoulders and started the car. "I'm sorry, Rhea."

Silent and stony, she stared out the window, her profile marbleized by the street light's bluish glare. At the rusty Bay Bridge, I didn't know where else to go, so I turned right and drove along the black waterfront street thinking, What a price for getting to bring her home! She'll probably never speak to me again.

The night was moonless and starless. To the left of the road and up a rise, a few houses along the beach glowed warmly, their tiny yellow squares hazy and distant. Inside people were watching television, reading, or whatever families do at ten o'clock on a Friday evening.

All I could think was, the words I'd practiced over and over were no good anymore.

Lowell might be right about this hurting her career. Wonder who influential was there tonight? Maybe they were going to buy. But no matter, I couldn't let him talk to her that way.

All this time, Rhea drank from the bottle, never saying a word, just staring out the window and chug-a-lugging.

When I parked the car in her drive, she jumped out and kicked off her shoes. Holding the champagne bottle by its neck, she stalked to the beach. I followed slowly. Even though she was about three yards ahead, I knew she was crying. What do I do now? Normally I melt when women cry, so tonight I'll probably just seep down into the sand and come out—Where is it they say you end up? Oh, yeah. China.

She kept right on going and hit the ebony water. The long, wet folds of her dress turned into weights. Sobbing and angry, she tugged at the material. In I go and grab her arm. "Stop, Rhea! It's too cold for this."

She jerked away and plowed farther out to sea. "I'm going for a swim, goddamnit!"

Up to her knees now, she's yanking at the dress and taking swigs from the bottle. She's soused, and I decided it's time to stop this craziness. I scooped her up. She draped her arms over my shoulders and nuzzled my neck. Wet from head to toe, we're both shivering, but I can feel her heart beating against my chest. For a minute, she looks up at me—her eyes the feathery, lavender color of a winter's sunset—and I'm not sure she knows where she is. The wind is blowing hard, but I heard her whisper, "Kiss me, Mike."

The instant I said, "You're mad at Lowell, Rhea," I knew I'd done wrong.

She leaped from my arms, gathered up the wet dress and

ran down the beach. "Go to hell, you bastard! Go to hell in a frigging fishing boat! Or better yet, go see about Lowell, just get the hell away from me!" For a minute I followed, then, like an idiot, I stopped, staring at her tiny silver shoes come alive in the sudden moonlight and listened to her yell. "Go straight to hell!"

Something I'm not even aware of happens when I'm around women these days. Alone too long, the psychologist would say. A dog's barking; probably coming to attack me. It's been one of those kind of evenings. Tired and confused, I take off my shoes, empty the water and follow.

I topped her steps and saw her crumpled in the doorway like a used, wet paper bag, but still swigging from that bottomless bottle. She sees me and mutters, her teeth chattering, "Goddamned men. Hate 'em."

"Let's go inside. You're freezing."

"Can't. Left my purse."

"Don't go away," I said teasingly, hoping to break through her anger. "I'll get my key."

I ran home. Inside, I rummaged in the kitchen drawer, throwing papers, a tire gauge, pliers, a coil of picture hanging wire all over the counter and cursing. A noise behind me made me stop and spin around. Swaying and shivering, Rhea stood inches away, her face streaked with tears. Her arms lifted. "Don't you know?" Stupidly, I shook my head. The faster my blood pumped, the louder my ears buzzed. She leaned against me, took my face in her hands and declared softly, "Sometimes I think they damaged your brain in that hellhole." My knees wanted to buckle. I felt her warmth through the wet dress, her lips moved against mine. "You still haven't figured it out?" Her hands ran through my hair, took control of my intellect, and I closed my eyes, deciding I didn't mind this sudden idyllic confusion.

Her kiss—even though I knew she was drunk—was the

most wondrous taste I'd ever tasted; it was sweet, it was tart, it was destruction and creation, but best of all, it was long. When we finally parted, she shifted back a step—I was leaning against the counter—and we stared at one another, breathing heavily. Her eyes sparkled, a hand reached out and brushed my forehead and she whispered, "Oh, Mike."

The words were there. "I love you, Rhea. You're part of me. I've loved you for so long, I think I thought I'd already told you. I'll take whatever you'll give, but I want you for my own. I'll wait for you or I'll go with you. I want to share dreams with you, days and nights with you. You breathed existence back into me and now I love you more than life, Rhea."

"Oh, Mike."

"If I have to wait forever, I will. All I want is to hear you telling me you love me too." I reached out and touched her face. Tears quivered in her eyes, and my own filled.

She grabbed my hand and kissed my palm. My heart beat became one long, continuous blow when her fingers flew from one stud on my shirt to the next, she slid her hands inside and kissed my chest.

I cradled her face, brushed her lips with mine, and into her mouth I whispered desperately, "I love you, Rhea!"

"I know."

More than touch, sight or sanity, I yearned to hear her say it, but I knew it really didn't matter if she'd just let me love her. "I want you."

"I know."

"Forever."

"Yes."

I waited. Through the fury of discarding clothes, through the research of her body, her study of mine, through the maze of lips, arms, eagerness, legs, muscle, union, sweat, tears of joy, and fulfillment, I waited.

Confession is good for the soul, I've heard, and later that

night, with more dialogue, intense exploration of her spirit, patience and the joy our bodies experienced simultaneously, the genesis of our love dawned as new as the morning we watched. Somewhere during that night, Rhea told me her secrets, her dreams, but most meaningful of all, she told me she loved me. She told me this declaration was new to her. Never before had she spoken the words I'd felt such unbelievable relief over hearing. Somewhere in her past—and I'll probably never know the source or the motive because she knows I'd go on a crusade and lay the heart of the matter at her feet—feelings died. But bring her alive again, we did.

Morning came, Randy called and I told him I was busy, to find another deck hand for a day or two. I fell back into her arms, trothing her my life, making her pledge me hers, and we slept.

The sun blinded me. I sat up in the bed and looked around. Was it all a dream? Oh, no! Had she really been here? That part I'm sure about. I glanced at the dream catcher tacked over my bed. "Thanks, pal. Finally, only the good ones got through," I remembered her kissing me good-bye, one last touch, but all real—very real.

From the open window, a soft breeze floated a scrap of paper off my desk. I threw back the cover and grabbed it mid-air. "I'll hurry back. I love you! R." it promised.

Our debate in the dark returned. Knowing I shouldn't, but burning with a new, insatiable fire, I'd begged her to cancel her New York trip. How long? Weeks? Months? I can't remember, and jumping up, I darted into the kitchen and opened the pantry door. On the big calendar, I search March's dates. Saturday, the twenty-third, "Rhea-NY," I'd scribbled while she'd nibbled on my ear. There's a number under the word "Plaza," but that's not what I'm looking for and I flip the page, then another and see in April's third block, "Rhea returns." Good God! That's forever away!

I dialed the number.

"Good morning! The Plaza. May I help you?"

"Yes, please leave a message for Rhea. She'll be arriving around mid-afternoon. What? No, it's just Rhea. Look on your book! Yes. That's her. Tell her to call Mike. She'll know. Write this down. I miss you. Hurry home. Love, Mike."

I'm late. Randy's going to be pissed, but he'll get over it. The big problem is I don't fall asleep until it's time to get up. No! The big problem is that for two and a half days I've been wondering what the hell's going on. She's driving me crazy! So is the man on the Plaza's desk. Said he didn't like my tone. Well, I'm tired of talking to him, too, but that's not the riddle here. What's wrong, Rhea? This old worn-out deck hand is gonna lose his job, but that's the least of my worries. Why hasn't she called?

Nine

Monday night, Rhea called. After she calmed me, saying now there was a touch of madness in my voice like she'd seen in my eyes occasionally, she explained her exhaustion, and I realized it rang true in her low voice. "What are they doing to you?"

"It's been a constant drive, drive. Note-taking half a day, painting in the afternoon and sometimes at night after their endless round of cocktail parties and dinners with inexhaustible speakers. When I have a break, it's either when you're out on the boat or in the middle of the night."

"For chrissakes, Rhea! I don't mind! I'd rather you call me in the middle of the night than not at all! Rhea, I want to come up for the weekend."

"Mike, I told you this would be intense. I'll be working on weekends too. There's no place for you to stay. I've got a roommate."

"I can check into a hotel near you. You can come when you…"

"Please try to understand, Mike, I'm blessed to have been chosen for this opportunity. This is something…" Listening to her credible excuse, and acknowledging my ineffective sympathy, my thoughts strayed to memories of her salty tears of ecstasy, her sweet-tasting mouth, and my covetousness only worsened, my room grew colder, and New York and Rhea seemed to occupy another planet. "…and I fall asleep the minute my head hits the pillow. Be patient, darling."

"Just tell me one thing…"

What I longed to hear, she said, making the dream reality, the distance shrink and the two days and nights we'd had in one another's arms, a poignant sliver of miracles to come. Further and further I pushed away ideas of long separations, telling myself our love would not be like this. No, its rhythm held awards; its music, stolen from heaven, sustained me. Our life would be sweet and sad, energizing and overwhelming, but such is the way of love. And being realistic, the more famous she becomes, the more she'll be gone, and I'll act testy and she'll get angry, but we'll always work it out and end up in each other's arms.

Yanking me back into the now, she wanted to hear every detail about my confrontation with Charlotte, if there had been more notes or pranks, and all about our charters. After bringing her up to date, I ended my dull list of activities by telling her I'd had dinner with Mom and Dad, that I'd started making kites again, and that Delilah would run up her steps when we'd go out walking as if to say, "Let's invite Rhea!" I never asked the one question nagging me: if she'd told Lowell about us.

Time inched by. At her house, I watered her scrawny plants and schemed: I'll tell her they're dying, and she'll come home! But I know better, and if I want her love, I mustn't trick her or beg or threaten. At that moment it also dawned on me that no matter how long I lived, getting used to her being gone would never be easy.

During our brief but intense time together, we'd said so many things. Words slid out like drops of melted wax flowing down the candles we burned, building and building. And then, there were those sacred times we'd forgotten to eat, forgotten to talk, forgotten to sleep. But what had she meant when she said, "…like when that madness flares up in your eyes"? Had I frightened her somehow? Well, at times, her ambition frightens me.

When I'm in her house, like now, memories swamp me, slightly deranging my mind. From her windows, I survey her beach, ocean and sky, and like a lovesick pup, I sit on the stool before her unfinished canvas and touch her paint brushes. I go to her closet to breath in her fragrance, stand at her dressing table and remember how she lifts her hair with both hands; she knows this little mannerism drives me berserk and she'd laugh naughtily when I'd grab her, crushing her to me.

Wandering about her rooms, I fondle her pottery and her books. Now she's left a book titled Peru open on her worktable. Like before, I kept her place and flipped the pages. There are no pictures. I shudder and wonder if she's really planning another trip this time. I miss her, wish she would come home and never leave me again, but remind myself what I must do with those overly-possessive thoughts. Unlike the norm, our life will ebb and flow and no matter what I want, I must accept, agree and even encourage her to do what she must.

But there's always the possibility we can go to Peru

together. If we're married...Wait! What had she said? A flippant, "We'll see." Mother of God! In the delirium of lovemaking did I ignore doubt and invent promise? But I didn't imagine she told me she loved me.

It's suddenly dastardly cold here. At least if she goes to Peru, and if she'll let me tag along it'll be warmer. Sometimes, I imagine I've been cold all my life; but I know it's an affliction left over from Korea.

In South America, during the day I'll be her protector while she stalks tigers and snaps pictures of monkeys. She'll be inspired and paint the uncivilized, lush jungles and its inhabitants, and I'll watch, ready to defend her honor until she rests. Then, stimulating her tired muscles, I'll taste her erotic honey, ravish her listless body until she's ready to scale mountains of passion, she'll come with me, and we'll escape to our own holy cities.

I sit down and read what she's underlined: "In the Peruvian Andes, stonework—tens of thousands of years old—has been found, so intricate it still inspires awe, and although it had yet to be named, engineering was born." Another page: "Mochica pottery..." Damnation, she is going to Peru! For pottery! ..."often depicts men dashing across a desert carrying pouches,...men's faces, arms and legs are drawn on the lima bean!" In spite of myself, I walked over and studied her pottery collection with new interest. No pots covered with bean-men, so she's not made this trip yet, and when she does, I'll follow.

Two more weeks pass. We talk—not enough—but we talk. I tick the days off the calendar and tell myself I'm in training.

Every day now, more people are out on the beaches. The weather's perfect, the fishing's good, but my life revolves around Rhea's calls.

Yesterday, an angler hooked my shoulder. Out of earshot,

Randy accused me of not paying attention, and he was probably right. My arm's sore, but more from the tetanus shot than the injury.

Then last night, after blithely sweet-talking me through the pitfalls of diametric careers, I lost it and shouted, "The hell you say!" when she announced she'd decided to go to Paris, adding another month to our separation. Loneliness fed my paranoia, and before long we were arguing hotly. Ultimately, she slammed the receiver down and the blow disconnected not only our voices, but my many promises to her and myself, and I knew I'd made a serious blunder. An eternity later, I realized she wasn't going to answer her telephone, no matter what I offered the operator, the desk clerk or the hotel manager. But as if tenacity were my middle name, I refused to believe what had happened: a silly lover's quarrel. I'd cooled down. She'd cool down, too.

The next evening, I rushed home and began calling. An exhaustive hour later, numb and shaken, I stumbled out to the porch to begin my waiting and praying odyssey. Staring at the slick, mottled water, I wondered what stroke of Fate brought two people face to face then ripped them apart? I left a million messages that evening, and while I sat there trying to unravel my dilemma, Natalie called and invited me to dinner. My excuse echoed bogus and now Nat's upset with me. I'm not in the mood to see anyone or be sociable. I've got to do something so I called Eastern and made reservations on a flight to New York for Thursday.

Pacifying my family, tonight I ate dinner with Natalie and Max. Tomorrow night, it's Randy and Diane, next it's Mom and Dad. I guess my restlessness and impatient air says it all because they sense something's up, and they're trying to help so I told them I'd be flying out in two days.

After I left Randy and Diane's cookout, I walked the

streets. I stopped and gazed into a store window. A shiny, red, heart-shaped pillow with a cut-out and glued-on felt eye winking at me, and for an instant I wanted to smash my fist through the glass and into Betty Boop's caricature, but then, over in a corner, a brightly colored straw hat caught my attention. Every few circles of straw changed into another vibrant color: red to blue to yellow to green to purple, and began all over again. On that night that seemed like years ago now, we'd loved, laughed and rolled in her white sheets and I'd asked her why the addiction to white. She'd stared coldly into space and told me, "Because there's so much sin in the world." Despite my long lecture on forgiveness, I knew she wouldn't wear the hat, but in my obsession I heard her voice saying, "You're good. You're very, very good—for me," and I wanted to give that sombrero to her.

Randy gave in to my nagging, and we got back to the harbor before the store closed, and now, sitting beside me on the truck's seat, the cheerfulness of it makes me grin. Acting like nothing's happened, I hoped that when I flew up it would make her laugh too.

One thing's good about all this silence. I'm remembering all her little quirks: When she's really laying paint on the canvas, she hunches over, rolls her head from side to side and frowns. She forgets to eat, to sleep, so obsessed by her project, but I think I understand. Whether I do or not, I know I'd sacrifice anything to be with her, to have her in my arms. She's my place to go, my song, my light. Please come home, Rhea. I need you!

It's dark out. Surely she's back in the hotel by now. I'll call, and if she doesn't take my call, and if the desk clerk says she hasn't checked out, I'm going anyway.

Rhea doesn't fly off the handle like this, but the desk clerk clearly said she'd left, and there's no forwarding address. What did I do or say that could be this bad? Doubt engulfs me, but without talking it through with her, I'm baffled! How can I find her? On the edge and helpless, I laugh and know there's nothing I can do until she makes up her mind to let me. I canceled my flight, flooding the airwaves with my plea. Call me, Rhea. Goddamnit, call me!

Another week and no word. Nothing makes sense. After all we've been through and knowing how much I love her, how can she get this huffed simply because I didn't want her to go to Paris. If she's trying to prove a point, she's succeeded. I just pray it isn't with Lowell. That's it! Lowell's behind this! No. This change is too drastic. Rhea's too smart to let Lowell manipulate her. There's only one answer. She's changed her mind, and thinking these thoughts, I'm going insane little by little!

Even though I'm exhausted, I promised Mom and Dad I'd come for Sunday dinner. About ten feet from my truck, I saw my tires were all flat. Cursing, I went back inside, called the folks and waited until Dad brought the three spares he rounded up.

While we changed the tires, he begged me to come stay with them until this mess blows over. Not wanting him to know it's been going on for six months, I thanked him and promised I would if it continued.

Mom's been to church, but now she's bustling about the kitchen in her Sunday dress, apron secure. The roast is in the oven covered with potatoes, carrots and perfect circles of onion. I know she's cut little incisions in the meat and poked a garlic bud in each slit. The whole house smells good enough to eat, and I can't remember when I did last. She folded the Sunday paper, laid it on the table for me and poured me a cup of coffee. Dad said he's going to the garage to "putter around" and to join him if I'd like.

Mom sighed and said since he's retired, his tools, neatly hung and clean, are what's saved their marriage. "He goes out, picks up a board and makes it into a pile of sawdust. After he sweeps that up, he takes the hedge clippers around back, but the shrubs are perfect. He needs a part-time job," Mom maintains, and I know she's right. "He's got too much time. Everything's been done and re-done."

I suggested he might be happier helping out at Port Hetty, and Mom says he and Julian get into a fight every time he goes there.

She seemed pleased when I promised to talk to Natalie and Max about finding something for him in the restaurant. No need to tell her Nat's mad at me, calls me a recluse every time I decline a dinner invitation. The thing is, experience has taught me Nat always has a plan. She suspects what's happened between me and Rhea and is busy trying to find me someone new.

Meanwhile, hands immersed in hot sudsy water, Mom's gazing out the kitchen window watching Dad oil the toolshed door. She says she'll never talk him into buying a new living room suite now and that maybe tomorrow she'll pin the pattern on that new lavender and pink floral and cut out a dress she doesn't need. We both know that after dinner tonight, Dad will flip from channel to channel, rustle the newspaper, ask me what I think about whatever's going on around the world while Mom leafs through her latest *Ladies Home Journal*.

Sighing, I stretched and poured me some more coffee. This time of the evening is my favorite and I'd like to go for a walk with Delilah romping alongside. The television blares. What is this world coming to? That sounds like a Dad-aphorism. They say you do that when you grow older; begin to sound like your parents.

I kissed Mom, thanked her for inviting me to dinner and went out to tell Dad thanks for helping with the tires. On the way home, I decided to go for a walk on the beach, parked, and there in the placid, ocean-front quiet, I tried to plan the rest of my life.

One morning two weeks later, I woke and found Tess snoring peacefully beside me. Not very proud of myself, I eased from the bed and surveyed the room. Empty beer bottles, a path of tossed off clothes, and a head to equal the magnitude of what I'd done, punished me. I donned an old pair of shorts, slipped outside and Delilah and I ran until I collapsed in a sweaty, retching heap.

We've got an early charter in the morning. I need to stop this tossing, gather some rational thoughts and sleep. Randy says we've got a forty-five minute run to where he'd heard the marlin were biting. I miss Rhea so goddamned much! There will be an hour and a half preparation, six hours solicitous pampering and two hours cleaning up the boat and storing gear afterwards. Doesn't leave much time or energy for fun, but that's all in the eye of the beholder. I like the job, the hard work, and some days I don't think about my POW days at all, but I haven't gotten to that point where Rhea's concerned. Busy hands and body, free spirit. Ha! That'll never happen until I find out why she had such a change of heart. At least the chores on the boat are rote; you see a need, you take care of it.

When is she going to call and make the aching stop? The worst I said was, "I'm crazy from missing and wanting you!" I didn't tell her she was selfish. Those were her words. But maybe I did get a little angry when she called me devouring and tyrannical, and I shouldn't have proclaimed her cold and calculating, but I'm sorry and I'm dying to tell her if she'll give me the chance. I'd been exhausted and looking forward to hearing her voice. She was tired and upset over falling behind on some project she'd poured her guts into. We should have hung up right then with simple good night's, and I love you's.

Today was one of those long Indian summer days when everything you try to anticipate happens and more. A customer's line broke inches from my grapple hook. Then, in ten to fifteen mile an hour winds and waves almost five feet high, a client got sick and the others were looking a little unripe. Randy headed in with hopes Plan B—wetting hooks near the channel buoy—would find some mackerel or small dolphin, but the weather followed us, and with everyone's stamina on the edge, I convinced him to give up.

We left the slip around twilight, foot-dragging tired, and Randy insisted I come home and let Diane make us some supper. Since my stomach was caressing my backbone, I agreed under the condition they wouldn't try to talk me into going out afterwards. Randy laughed, and promised he had no intentions of letting her drag us into town.

Over the last weeks Diane appointed herself my personal matchmaker and I'd let her fix me up with enough tall, thin, short, fat, silly and serious Saturday night dates to last a lifetime. For a while I didn't even mind the heavily perfumed, stiffly sprayed hairdos or buying beer for their hollow legs. They were diversions. But real soon I got tired of them talking about clothes, who hit who last night or who's after who even though they're just a little bit married, plus it didn't take long before they realized I disappeared whenever they talked about settling down and having kids. Now, mostly they leave me alone while I drink beer and wonder if I'll ever see Rhea again, but tonight Diane's got another burlesque beauty queen she's wanting me to call.

"No, Diane!"

"But Mike, Natalie and Max are coming. Char and Julian are coming…"

"That's fine, but you're not inviting someone for me!"

"Then you do it!"

"Why can't we just have a quiet family get-together?"

"All you do is eat canned soup or spaghetti, drink beer and fall asleep watching TV. That's no life!"

"Says who?"

"Randy, talk some sense..."

"Leave me out of this," Randy insisted, burying his face in his new *Argosy*.

"It's either my way or not at all," I promised. Diane stormed from the room, and I left.

The phone was ringing when I got home. I dove for it like a starving sea gull after a crumb of bread. On the other end, Tess cooed, said I sounded lonely and thought she should come over. When we hung up, I knew she was bewildered, but she really only makes it worse.

Diane's right. At midnight, I woke to a fuzzy, crackling screen. I crawled into bed on top of the covers, then I couldn't sleep. I lay there remembering the first time Rhea joined me on the beach. Surprised to hear someone calling my name, I looked around to see her racing barefoot across the sand, loose shirt pressed against her full, bouncing breasts, long tanned legs pumping, her body in a slow, graceful twist. On the beach, winter or summer, she wears no shoes, and not much else. But as long as I live, I'll remember her slender toes in the sand, and their unpainted, shell-pink nails.

That was so long ago. That evening we'd talked like long-separated friends catching up on years in-between; about beach life, ocean life, and life. Afterwards, to meet several times a week at twilight became the routine more than the happenstance.

I'd started working for Randy and I'd hurry home, shower and sometimes brazenly knock on her door. One evening I remember in particular, she answered, a double crease between her brown birds-feather eyebrows and I'd gotten my first "Sorry, I'm busy." Crushed, I'd rammed my hands into my pockets, turned and ambled down the steps. She'd called out to my back, "I'm painting. I'm onto something good and just can't stop. See you tomorrow, okay?"

I said, "Sure thing," but wanted to take a long, slow walk into Camelot, not cherishing another admonishing like that again, but the very next evening, she joined me, getting my hopes up again. Our conversation was worthwhile, our mood light and easy. Then, several days passed and I didn't see any life at her place. It didn't take long for me to realize she'd left town. This time I felt rejected because she hadn't mentioned taking a trip, and I realized I wasn't as big an item in her life as I hoped.

Thursday night I saw a light in her window. Afraid of pushing, the next morning on my way to work, and to keep from being told "No" or breaking her train of thought, I left a note taped to her door welcoming her home and asking for a "walk" date.

When I got home, a note fluttered on my screen saying, "You're on! See you at 7!"

What happened then was that as the months passed, I sensed a shift from the simple friendship to a vital esteem—at least with me. I had no clue what was happening with Rhea, if anything.

Wanting more, I asked if I could watch while she painted. She'd answered, "No, but you can sit in the window-seat, and we can talk." I jumped at that.

Well, it seemed now that as far as she was concerned, the house, the beach and I no longer existed or mattered.

Randy hasn't booked a customer Saturday which means I can't put back as much this month, but what the hell am I saving for—a European tour? Not likely. Anyway, I needed to tighten the screen door, it drags and won't close all the way and flies and mosquitoes invade, making my life more miserable. And the truck needs an oil change and washing, and if I just can't do anything else outside, I'll go for a swim in the hottest part of the day, come inside and vacuum the floors and mop the kitchen. It's pretty sticky; spots have dog hair growing from them.

Maybe I'll call Natalie and Max and see if they'd like to go to Biloxi, see a movie, or get a hamburger and a beer or go dancing or all of it. It may be too late. The sun's already pretty low so it must be close to six, but what can they say except "Yes" or "No."

There was no answer at Nat's, and later I found myself at the looped drive, where we'd lived on County Road number something or other—the sign at the point reads D'Iberville Drive now. The cabins are gone. A smooth green carpet rolls from the black asphalt down the point to the reeds. Curly gray moss hangs in lacy tendrils from the scrub oaks. After the reeds end, the rippled, brackish water weaves sinuously to the next point, around a bend and becomes lost in the marsh, cyprus and pines.

Here, almost twenty-six years ago, my father handed me the .22 Remington and said, "Mike, don't take another step. There's a moccasin hiding just under that log. Shoot him in the head, right now. Aim for his beady eyes."

I released the safety, braced the gun against my shoulder, sighted the flicking tongue and squeezed. The butt recoiled brutally and my shoulder stung and a headless, speckled whip thrashed in the leaves, reflexes boiling. "Great shot, son! I wasn't sure you saw it." My father slapped me soundly on the already tender shoulder then marched toward the narrow pier, and stepped into the boat, straddling the wooden slat that served as a seat. He reached for the motor's pull cord and jerked the faithful little Evinrude into a sputtering, gurgling action. "Coming, Mike?" he asked impatiently.

"Yes, sir." I untied the slip knot, tossed the rope into the bow and jumped in, rattling oars and knocking over the bait can.

"Grab it, son, quick, or we might as well cut the motor! Can't fish without bait."

I righted the can. Black and brown crickets skittered and leaped in all directions. Finally recapturing all I could find, Dad told me to sit down and be quiet, that I had scared the fish away within a hundred miles. "By the way, that gun's yours."

As though the words still hung in the air, I remembered replying, "Sir?" but all I could think of was: Charlotte will kill me! Relentlessly, she'd begged our father to teach her to shoot, and one night we camped out in the back yard and she told Natalie, Randy and me, she just knew Dad planned to give that .22 to her for her birthday. But he didn't, and she never forgave him, and probably not me either. And now, just like when I'd ended up with the gun, she would like to kill me with icy hatred.

Regressing again, my dad, the mind-reader, had said, "Your sister's gonna be miffed. Think she had her eye on that gun." I told my father that it should be Charlotte's, wanting it desperately but dreading my sister's wrath more, but Dad insisted I earned it by clobbering that cottonmouth.

We'd fished silently, puttering back to the pier late in the day, and beneath a fuzzy, windswept sky, stood side by side at the long cleaning table. I watched my father gut, scale and fillet the mullet, cleaving the fish with such precision, I knew the knife's elaborate scrimshaw handle must be enchanted in his hand. He told me to toss the scraps into the murky water. I watched the water churn and turn pale with air bubbles. Wide-eyed, I asked what caused the commotion. Dad told me, and careful to conceal my terror, I dreamed about prehistoric eels and vampiric fish with red eyes gorging on chunks of flesh. I never swam off our pier the whole time we lived on the inlet.

But that day in particular, I followed my father into the kitchen and while we washed the fish, I begged my mother to start cooking, declaring starvation sat like death on my shoulders. She'd smiled, set the cast iron skillet on the stove and taken down her ready can of flour and meal mixture. In all sincerity, my empty stomach set up a genuine howl just thinking about her light hush-puppies, her cold, tangy slaw and a platter of crisp fish. I turned to wash up and bumped into Charlotte. Instructed to help, she glared at the fillets, whirled and asked why she hadn't been allowed to go. I prayed silently, "Please, God, don't let Dad say anything about the gun," fifty times before anyone said a word, but Dad shoved the worshipped gun into my hands, ordering me to clean it at once and store it away. I should have run screaming from the room and maybe Charlotte would have taken pity. Instead, I obeyed.

In my sister's eyes this had been admission to conspiracy, and to this day I could hear Charlotte, the wronged, exploding. "It's not fair! Kip always gets..." Leaving the room, I saw big tears flooding her cheeks, heard my mother, the peacemaker, soothing her child's wrath, and my father, the rabble-rouser, making matters worse when he told Charlotte her place was in the house, helping her mother.

On the staircase, I listened a few minutes while my parent's argued the pros and cons of Charlotte's duties and what they'd decided should be her future. In the end, Mother would buy her a new dress—that would make most girls happy—and some new hair ribbons and shoes: the whole smear.

"Time she acted more like a young lady instead of hanging around with her brothers and their friends anyway," Dad added, stacking the last humiliating stone on her ailing femininity. In my head, Dad's words rang clear and I realized no one really understood Charlotte and I felt sad for her then, as I did now.

Before daylight that morning, when my father shook my shoulder telling me it was time to get up, I'd thought about suggesting we take Charlotte, but forgot, hurrying to catch up when the screen door banged behind Dad. Why I barely had time to grab the cheese toast and the shiny, red apple Mother thrust in my hands!

And that night, guilt petrified me at the dinner table; the mouth-watering food stuck in my throat. At one point, I hoped Dad would change his mind, but wanted to keep that gun as bad as a ten-year-old could want anything, so I kept my mouth shut.

For days afterwards, with her turbulent blue eyes downcast, Charlotte would pass me as though I were invisible. Nothing I said or did, down to offering her my favorite taw marble with the twisted ribbons of orange and blue petrified deep inside, could thaw her cold hostility.

Back in my car, I wondered if Charlotte would give me another chance, why wouldn't Rhea? So far, Charlotte and I were in good shape, but for the life of me I hadn't a clue how to change the wretchedness between Rhea and me, and I craved her approval so much more.

Ten

I parked in Charlotte's driveway, ran my hand over the smooth leather case on the seat beside me and wondered how she would react. Whether she threw it, along with curses and me out the door, or cuddled it like a long lost friend and cried, I'd experienced enough uneasiness forehand to minimize any healthy tantrum. And with Charlotte, it could go either way.

My first surprise, finding the rifle still in the top notches of the gun rack in my old room, proved fascinating enough. After I oiled and cleaned it, I sat for a long time in the dim room with it resting across my knees, feeling its weight and sensing its energy. I had almost forgotten the incident. Revisiting first with Charlotte's comment, and later by myself on my time-warp visit to the old homesite, the incident returned as fresh as yesterday. Now as never before, I appreciated Charlotte never excusing my easily earned ownership. She deserves the rifle after waiting so long, and maybe, just maybe therein lies the root of her anger. Time to mend those fences, hopefully end the short, fidgety visits, soothe her eyes so full of loathing, and collect my reward: a smile.

Although still pleasing to my eyes, I glanced around at Gramma Kipling's tumbling down, gingerbread house. Seeing its sagging roof, its peeling paint, its once blossom-flushed yard now lost to creeping, savage vegetation, I saw Charlotte and Julian had plenty to concern them, not to mention one active toddler and another inquisitive five-year-old. And according to Dad, Julian's lack of presence at home and on the job didn't help much. When I had been declared MIA, Dad had no recourse other than to move Julian into my slot though aware his son-in-law never demonstrated much interest in the seafood business. Dad said he counted on the princely salary and the fact that Charlotte was his daughter snagging Julian's attention and giving the position a bit more respect. To his disappointment, Julian turned out worse than he had anticipated. He would vanish for hours and when he did parade in, he would sit in his office either on the phone or reading the newspaper.

Years passed, and according to Mom, Dad gradually shouldered more and more of the responsibilities he intended the holder of that position to manage. Then, last year, Dad began having arm and chest pain and his doctor made three recommendations: surgery—which Dad adamantly refused—hire more help, or retire. Hating to see the company fold, Dad swallowed the bitter pill of acquiescence and did what he must. Consequently, his retirement coupled with Julian's sloppy business style now required two assistants to perform one's obvious but indifferently viewed tasks. It seemed no matter what degree of badgering or humoring Dad attempted, there had been no alternative. Mom's insinuations left no doubt that she hoped I would march in and reclaim my old job. Sound as her intentions were, my better judgment told me to tread carefully, and try as I might, I came up with no diplomatic suggestions with which to approach Julian without whacking him on the head with my plans. But regardless of the awkward abyss between Julian and myself, I made up my mind to give Charlotte the rifle as a peace-offering. I had even prepared a subtle little speech about helping with the household repairs.

Charlotte paused on the way to the front door, wiping her hands on a bright tea towel, at first smiling hesitantly, but then she rushed to unhook the screen. "Kip, what a nice surprise! You look great."

Things were looking up. She had not called me by my nickname since my return. "Thanks." I wanted to hug her but she wheeled briskly and I followed her into the tidy, but Spartan kitchen.

Sonny sat in his high chair picking tiny cubes of cheese and broken crackers from his tray and eyed me suspiciously. The kid doesn't remember me, I mused, squatting to feed the baby a bite and tousling his golden hair. I should come more often in spite of the usual cold receptions from my sister, but making the infant's ambivalence seem trivial, Shallie leaped from the floor where an instant before I spied her coloring laboriously in her quiet determined, five-year-old way and locked her small arms about my neck. Bringing her with me, I rose, Shallie shrieking in my ear. I unlocked her hands, twirled her in my arms and she rewarded me with a wet kiss on the cheek.

With Shallie on my knee, I told Charlotte she and Julian made beautiful children. She blushed, and I felt content seeing she was still capable of feelings.

I picked up the rifle case from where I laid it on the floor and set it on the kitchen table. "Charlotte, this is for you, if it's not too late." A frown deepened her forehead, shadowing her deep-set eyes. "If it is, save it for Shallie or Sonny, or maybe Julian would like to have it."

Charlotte cut her eyes to the case without touching it and moved to a large tin with red tulips, pried off its lid and placed cookies on a pink flowered plate. "I baked tea cakes today. Shallie mashed the raisins in and you look like you could use a dozen or two." She bustled around the kitchen, putting the coffee pot into action, getting out cups, spoons and finally, setting the plate of cookies on the table. I started to confront her about the rifle, but her voice, high and edgy, broke through my apprehension. "I've been meaning to ask...Are you going back into the Air Force?"

"No. I've bought the beach house I've been renting. And I like being outside, so I'll just keep working with Randy." When I pulled out a chair for Charlotte, I could have sworn I heard her expel a deep sigh. Settling back, Shallie still glued to my knee, I reached over, patted my hands together before Sonny and said, "Wanna come sit with me and Shallie?"

The child's brown eyes grew enormous, his bottom lip quivered and he whimpered, "Mommy?"

"Char, I think he's about to cry. I don't remember him being that timid."

"He just woke up. Go ahead and pick him up."

I lifted the passive little boy who watched me closely. "Hey, remember me. I'm Mommy's brother," I said gingerly. The baby stared at me, at Shallie and at his mother. When he rolled his big eyes back to my face, I detected a hairbreadth of softening.

"Just remember he's only eighteen months old and he hasn't seen you for a while now. Give him a cookie."

As usual, Charlotte's shrewd choice of words drove home her point. She knew damned well I didn't feel welcome, that she and Julian had been anything but friendly, but I suppressed all those observations and did as she instructed.

Sonny crammed the whole cookie in his mouth and gooey crumbs showered all over. I pretended to grab them, making a gobbling noise, and the baby grinned. Then I threw several crumbs into the air and tried to catch them with my open mouth, holding Sonny and Shallie tight while I bobbed around. The little boy giggled and said, "More." Charlotte set a plastic cup on the table beside us and after we devoured the cookie together, I handed the youngster the cup. Sonny sucked hard, sighed loudly and milk ran out his mouth, down his bibbed outfit and onto my pants leg. I had to bite my lip to keep from laughing over his cunning. Charlotte handled the scolding for me, as I knew she would. Then Sonny offered me the cup and I pretended to drink. The toddler giggled.

"Well, it's the sort of thing you must do regularly, but I think you've got the idea," Charlotte murmured. "Now, tell me what I'm supposed to do with this." She pushed the rifle case a few inches toward me.

I wiped the baby's face, shirt and my leg with the wet cloth Charlotte supplied and asked Sonny, "Want me to take you for a walk on the beach?"

Shallie looked up and said brightly, "I do!"

"Sure, Sister can come too, can't she, Son?" Begrudgingly, the baby shook his head. This time I threw back my head and laughed. It felt good, and I couldn't remember when I'd done it last. "Sure she can. We'll all go. Even Mommy if she wants too."

"Mike, you haven't answered my question. Besides, it's Sonny's nap time."

"Aw, come on, Char. I haven't seen these kids in ages. And as for the rifle, you've waited long enough, too, you tomboy you."

"I don't have time to be a tomboy anymore. I don't have time for anything remotely resembling play. Unlike you,

I have obligations, including meals to cook, clothes to wash—"

"Then let me help. I'll take them for a walk and when we get back, I'll do whatever you want. Cook, wash—"

"You're not funny. And you'd just be in the way."

"Boy, you really hate me, don't you? Go ahead, tell me what's eating at your insides, Char. Don't you think it's time we cleared the air between us. I'd like a chance to get to know your kids, and with a little luck, maybe you."

"What's that supposed to mean?"

Starting with the rifle episode, I unloaded, and for the first time, realized there had been a huge gap between our youth and my return. "Most siblings weather their fights and occasionally turn into friends. That's what I want." I went on to say I'd seen enough war and suffering to last any mortal forever, admitted I craved peace, was weary of butting heads with her and asked her forgiveness for whatever it was I had done. Lastly, I added she didn't even have to tell me if she didn't want to, but my gut feeling was that she ached to yell at me, to curse me.

We sat in strained silence for a few minutes, even the children quietly amused themselves with their snack as if they knew I needed badly to hear whatever their mother might say. "There is one thing, Mike." I waited. "I'm sorry about what I said that day—about the children you wanted to adopt. I didn't know the whole story."

In one swift movement, I let the children slide to their feet, reached out and hugged my sister. She flung her arms around my neck and sobbed. "And I'm glad you're alive!" She cried for a while longer, then, like she had collected, stored, arranged and rearranged words all her life for a letter to me she'd never written, she overflowed. Not only had I taken her rifle, I'd stolen her best friend, Mandy. Then, in her mind, I died before she could make amends for her injustices. Through her tears she described her mixed feelings when I returned from the grave, elated to see me alive, but fearing I would claim Gramma's house and Julian's job. Saddened by my more obvious abuse—scars and gauntness—she had been horrified listening to the psychiatrist depict my mental anguish and grieved when I begged to see Mandy. But far outweighing her wish to patch our estrangement, she feared for herself and the children's welfare to the point of obsession.

Poor Charlotte. What turmoil she had suffered. She seemed relieved when I told her what a big part she, Natalie and Randy played in my survival. I asked her if she remembered the four of us fighting over whose turn was next for the one record player we'd owned. When she laughed, I relaxed. Then she asked if I had bought each of us a package of those plastic discs for our 45 rpm records as a bribe. I grinned and told her, no, I did that because she never would lend me any.

She sat back in her chair, a new tide of tears washed her face and she murmured, "Oh, Mike, how awful I've been!"

After reassuring her as best I could, I concluded with, "Except for the written threats and voodoolike happenings, my life has been quiet and happy until…" Here she stopped me and demanded to know what I was talking about. I cited specifics, and when astonishment struck her face, eliminating another, and more personal suspect, I sighed.

Overcoming her confusion, she probed, "What else has happened? You were about to tell me more."

Briefly, I described Rhea's evasiveness, omitting the romantic part. At that point, Charlotte apologized for her outburst after meeting Tess on my birthday. She referred to my subsequent visit to her house at which time she'd accused me of making up for lost time with nurses, Randy's customers, barmaids, and Rhea, sarcastically proposing we should call Edward R. Morrow who had interviewed me after my debriefing, to vouch for my speedy readjustment to life, but hurting me worse that day, she'd repeated in great detail Mandy's suffering. But now she's offering her support. I thanked her, declaring I would accept if I knew where Rhea was, and shrugging off my despair, I offered, "Why don't you go shopping, visit a friend, or go for a ride. Tell me what's next for the kids. I'll stay as long as you need."

"I do have some errands I could run."

"Then go." I nodded at the children expectantly. They headed toward me, two hands slipped into mine and four big eyes looked up. "We'll walk first, then Shallie can help me put Son down for his nap."

Charlotte sighed heavily. "That would be nice. I'll be back in an hour."

"Take your time, Char." Ignoring her long gaze, I sent Shallie for toys. She returned with a red plastic bucket and two yellow shovels, and the three of us headed for the front door.

Outside, I lifted Sonny to my shoulders. His feet bounced against my chest as we walked. "Hold on tight, Son." He leaned over my head and gripped my chin with two sticky hands. I inhaled the pungent air deeply and headed for the beach. "Ummm, you guys notice how good the air smells? Nothing smells quite like sea air. What does it remind you of, Shallie?"

"Fish."

"Me, too," Sonny chimed.

Later in the upstairs bathroom, I washed their faces and hands, gave them a drink of water and Sonny said, "Potty." I looked at Shallie wide-eyed, asked her to excuse us and Sonny and I gathered around the commode. Somewhere I'd read you're supposed to praise the success, so I did and the pink-cheeked little boy beamed when I helped him untwist and pull up his underwear. Then the three of us climbed on Sonny's bed and I read them two Dr. Seuss books. I pulled up a pink and blue afghan I could have sworn Gramma had crocheted, and we all fell asleep.

Sonny woke me digging in my eyes. "Get up, Unk Mike. Let's play." Shallie sat up and said, "Can I have the rifle, Uncle Mike?"

"That's for your parents to decide."

We scampered downstairs to find Charlotte lugging in sacks of groceries. When I brought in the last bag, she asked how it went and smiled when I answered, "Great!"

Shallie, dragging a sack of potatoes, told her mother we took a long, long nap and could she please, please have the rifle.

My sister stared at me with surly eyes. I shrugged my shoulders and told her what I told her daughter, and I could tell she wavered. After she gave the children a glass of orange juice she told them to go out back and play for a while, and then she busied herself putting up canned goods and filling pots with beans and peeling potatoes. Suddenly, she turned, said she would like very much to have the rifle, and I hugged her hard.

Julian, who I had not seen but once since my return, walked in the back door, barely said "Hello," and asked what was for supper. Charlotte told him pork chops, green beans and boiled potatoes. Julian cussed, opened the refrigerator door, snatched out a beer, then slammed the door especially hard, rattling its contents. He leaned against the kitchen sink and took a long swig. Rude pig, I thought. Didn't even offer me one. But then he spat out something about "troublemaker." Charlotte wouldn't look up from cutting vegetables and I decided I had better leave. I rose, said I enjoyed my visit and headed for the back door.

"Don't forget that damned thing!" Julian bellowed, noisily throwing his empty bottle into the trash near the back door.

Glaring at Julian, I said, "Charlotte wants it."

"No, she doesn't. It's dangerous having guns around children."

Watching my sister shrink, I saw fear shroud her body like a weighted net. Obediently, she shook her head, Julian snatched up the case and shoved it into my hands. Then he whirled, yanked the refrigerator door open and pulled out another beer.

"Okay. Thanks for the cookies and coffee, Char. Nobody makes coffee like you, except maybe Gramma and..."

"Damnit to hell, Mike, we're all aware your grandmother's dead. So's your grandfather. Do you think we'd be living here if they weren't?"

Charlotte sucked in her breath. She nor Julian would look at me. "I guess not."

Troubled about my sister's unhappiness, I walked down the hallway and out the front door, suddenly remembering the children. By the time I rounded the back corner to tell them good-bye, Julian and Charlotte were shouting at each other. I tried not to listen, but my name broke through their heated words several times, along with the word "inheritance." After I hugged the kids, I slipped around the side of the house farthest from the back door, got in my truck and drove away, hoping Charlotte would tell Julian what I'd said and put his mind at ease.

By the time I got home, it was getting dark. Two or three stars were already visible and a milky half-moon reflected on the sand, mirroring in the water. Charlotte's dilemma lingered on my mind. Just like Dad said, it almost seemed that any attempt to ease their predicament only worsened my sister's situation.

Out of habit, I glanced at Rhea's house. Her lights were on! But even in my excitement, I noted several cars were in her driveway, so I guessed I had better stay away. Hopefully, she would see my lights, too, and join me when her company left.

Anxious to see her, hold her and kiss her, I almost forgot the awkward time lapse since we'd last talked. When it hit me, I paced, stopping to glance at her house from time to time. An hour passed. I opened a beer, noticed my hands trembled when I cut several slices of cheese, and tried to decide if I should ask why she hadn't called, inquire about Paris or wait for her to start the conversation. Tossing the empty aside, I made up my mind to pay her a visit when her guests left. Another hour and four beers later, I glanced at the untouched plate of cheese and crackers, walked out onto the deck and stared at her dark house.

Mildly inebriated, borderline crazy and gravely wounded, I staggered inside, read a line or two in the book she'd given me on Zen and flung it aside, ready to fly across the sand. Why didn't she come? Stubbornness? Apathetic? How could that be after what we'd shared! Then why don't I go? I'll admit to bull-headedness, but complete frustration repeatedly yanked my senseless, animal self back into the room. I picked up the book on Senator Estes Kefauver and his Special Committee to Investigate Organized Crime, drank another beer, and threw the empty across the room.

Eleven

From the moment Natalie walked in asking about my well-being, I knew her surprise visit would go sour. I denied a problem, asked her what she referred to and she answered, "You're off-balanced gait." I reminded her I was somewhat cripple, but admitted I'd been celebrating Rhea's return and invited her to join me. With that, she stormed up, set her hands on her hips and glared at me, and I almost laughed knowing how hard she tried to look and sound like Mother. "You're no more a cripple than I. Your biggest affliction is self-pity." Her eyes narrow slits, she continued, "What would make you do this stuff? You're the luckiest of us all."

"Ha!" I jeered, wanting to remove her bodily and stop the

predictable outburst. Instead I dug deeper into the sofa's cushions and practiced tuning her out, but couldn't resist adding, "Much more 'luck' and I'll be throwing myself a party!"

"Everyone loses something along life's way. Some more, some less. But you'd gotten your life back on track, and you're healthy—or at least you were. Who knows now? And that beautiful, talented woman next door loves you—God only knows why!"

"Sez who?!"

"I'm not deaf and dumb. And she would probably admit it if you'd act your age, clean up your act and make an effort to find out what is wrong between you two. But, no! What do you do? Smoke a little 'pot' and booze it up big time. Wanna know how else I know? Whenever she's around, your face goes all mushy—not nasty like it is right now. Your smile howls 'spellbound,' lacks reason and your eyes stick to her like you're her servant. But you… you'd rather spend your time sitting over here blocking out the world. Seems I gave you too much credit… I should have know better than to feel so proud of you since…"

"What you're saying, little sister, is I'm a bastard."

"You're getting warm. What happened to those grandiose ideas for Dad's business? And what about the guy who wanted to go to Law School, maybe into politics, help the needy, take the underdog's case? He pouts! Nearing comatose, he's frying his brain, or whatever that stupid stuff does, and he looks somewhat ill, I'd say—even more than when I saw him in the hospital.

"Oh, Mike! Don't you know there are people who care about you? Your whole family waits for your next move, while you just sort of drift from one gloomy phase to another."

My head throbbed. Ready for some peace and quiet, I had run out of patience and wanted her out of my house.

Making her mad might be my only salvation. "What's your point, Nat?"

During her speech, noticing my mouth was drier than dirt, I pushed up from the sofa and headed for the refrigerator. She followed. I grabbed another beer and opened it. Before I knew what happened, she'd snatched it from my hand and threw it against the wall. "Hey! I guess you know you're gonna have to clean up that mess!"

She wheeled and headed for the door. Over her shoulder she shouted, "Clean it up yourself! What little I've done doesn't make a dent in this sty. And while you're wallowing in this piggish pity, might I add, if you'd done this shitty stuff right after you were found, that would have been one thing, but why now? Precocious Kip, we used to say. What a joke!"

"Are you finished?"

"Yes!"

"Good. I'd like you to leave."

She froze. Her eyes darted across my face and her mouth bunched up. "No, by damn! Not until you to tell me what's happened!" Marching back into the room, she plopped down in the butterfly chair, crossed her arms and steamed fearlessly.

"That's something I'd like answered too!" I snarled, jamming my face close to hers. "Since you're on such good terms with the lady next door, find out why she got upset when I told her I didn't want her to go to Paris right after…"

"What?"

"Hells bells, I thought you knew everything!"

"I only know what I've seen. Have you tried…"

"Yeah! She won't talk to me. She won't see me. So you see, Nat, I'm willing, but we've got this little communication problem." I'd taken my sister's arm, pulled her up and led her to the door, opened it and pushed her outside. "So you be my goodwill ambassador. Go over and fix it for me, will ya?" I slammed the glass between us, whirled and headed for the refrigerator.

The door opened, she stepped back inside, got her purse and turned to leave. "You sarcastic ass. No wonder she won't listen."

The telephone rang. I turned on the television, dropped onto the sofa and gulped my new beer. She moved around in front of me. The longer I sat and let it ring, the bigger her eyes got. "What if it's Rhea!" she cried. "Aren't you going to answer it?"

"Help yourself."

She snatched up the receiver, muttered hello and looked at me, the color draining from her face. "When, Mom?" I finished my beer, leaned over, put the empty on the table and plopped back into the cushions. "Don't worry! Mike and I are on our way," she promised and hung up.

"I'm not going anywhere"

"Dad's had a heart attack. They're taking him to Biloxi by ambulance. He's asking for you. Get up!" Through the doorway and without looking back, she yelled, "Come on, Mike!"

When they finally let me in his room, I felt sick when I saw all the tubes, the oxygen tent and Dad's ashen face. For the first time I believed the doctor. He's not going to make it! I pulled a chair to his bedside and found his cold hand under the covers. "Dad, it's Mike. Come on, Dad. Look at me." The sheets barely moved with his feeble breathing; his eyelids, and his whole body looked like marble. "Don't do this, Dad," I begged. "You're too young. Fight, Dad. Fight, damnit!"

A nurse took his hand from mine, laid it across his chest and touched my shoulder. When I looked up, she shook her head. People in white entered the room and pushed the tent away. At the door, I looked back in time to see them pull the sheet over his serene face.

In a small room down the hall, Mom sniffed and dabbed her eyes with a handkerchief. I sat down by her and took her hand. "He had something he wanted to tell you, Mike."

"I'm sorry, Mom. We got here as quick as we could."

"I know." She scanned the room coolly. "Where's Julian?"

"He's with the kids, Ma," Charlotte offered weakly. "Someone had to stay with the kids."

Mom rose, turned to me, dry-eyed, and for a moment I detected a glint of anger. To be expected, I guessed. "We have a problem, Mike." She swung around. "Randy, you and the girls see if there's anything else that needs to be done here." She spun back to me. "I'd like you to take me home now, Mike." She stuffed her tissues into her purse and snapped it shut. The crack reverberated around the room like a gunshot. She took my arm and drew me along. Together, we walked from the tense, silent room and headed down the hall, leaving behind opened-mouthed stares.

Natalie ran up and asked if they could come. Mom looked at her blankly, glanced at her watch and said in an hour or two. Indignantly, Nat asked me if I was sober enough to drive. She'd seen me swilling coffee and I was about to tell her I was a clear-headed cretin when Mom spoke up, "Doesn't matter. I'm driving."

At the house, Mom placed a cup of steaming coffee before me and set Dad's Wild Turkey bottle beside it. "From the looks of you, you could use this."

Regardless of what everyone thought, I'd sobered quickly on the way to the hospital, and now accepted her offer readily. From the moment we entered her car, she talked non-stop about the business and Julian's mishandling of funds after Charlotte persuaded her father into making him Business Manager. It seemed Dad spent the last three years trying to convince Julian he didn't know how to run the company, making Dad's job of straightening out the mess twice as maddening. Then there had been a huge argument, ending with both men raging at one another. For the next day and a half, my father had poured over the books, discovering bankruptcy conclusive. Consequently, Dad fired Julian two nights ago. "If Julian had pulled the trigger of a gun pointed at your father's head, he couldn't be more guilty for his death."

"That's pretty drastic, Mom."

"You won't think so when you know all the facts. Your father spent all his life building this business—and a self-respecting reputation—and he hoped you would come around soon, wanting back in. I believe that's what he wanted to tell you." Calmly, she took my hand, watched me closely and said, "Mike, I want you to take over. You don't have to answer this instant, but working for Randy can't be much of a challenge. Some day soon you'll be bored with that. And while we're on that subject... Haven't you wondered where Natalie and Max got the money for that swanky restaurant and Randy, that flashy boat? Charlotte's suffering, but we all know why: Julian's gambling.

"You look surprised, Mike!"

"I knew Charlotte was miserable. I didn't know about Julian's gambling, but, Mom, if you're referring to Gramma and Grandad's inheritance, I do know all about that."

She sighed deeply and paced the room. "Are you going to ask for your share?"

For the first time, I noticed my mother's straight back seemed a little more stooped, her thick hair more white than dark and deep lines at her eyes and the corners of her mouth. She had been a dark beauty in her day—I had seen pictures of her and Dad in younger times—and she had only gained some roundness where before there was flat and thin. Her eyes never lost the twinkle I remembered seeing in those pictures, though. Dad had added a slight paunch and lost two-thirds of his hair, but remained handsome and strong—until today. But during the last few hours, I'd come to admire Mom's composure. With Dad's passing, my mother shifted into a sturdy but genteel bravado, and I found myself a little in awe. "No. It's too late, Mom."

"Mike, you should know your father and I love you dearly, but son, you've been living like an ostrich. We were giving you a chance to catch up. Well, in my book, you did a remarkable job of adjusting, but something's gone awry. I don't know what and I'm not asking you to tell me unless you want to. Just remember, I'm here.

"As far as your brother and sisters are concerned, I think you are being most charitable, but if that is your final decision, I'll abide by it.

"Now, please snap out of whatever you're bogged down in and lend me a hand. There's work to be done if you're interested. I'm too angry to grieve right now; there will be time for that later."

On a dismal April day, we buried Dad. My mother, dressed in black, wept softly and leaned against my shoulder only once during the whole ceremony. I knew she'd been Puritan-like in matters of family, devotion, education and the Bible, but I'd never seen her put to the test before. She grieved but regally. Not even the tireless Eleanor Roosevelt, my mother's idol, could have matched Mother's performance dealing with Dad's death, dispensing duties to the rest of the family and diving into the business.

Julian did not attend the funeral, but I learned later Mom forbid his presence, but the remainder of our family stood by as solemn as the day.

When we left the grave side, I spotted Rhea and my heart skyrocketed. Had she come for me, or for my family? My question was soon answered. She disappeared as quickly as she'd come.

In the days that followed, my brother, sisters and I spoke of immediate issues only. Dad's will transferred the business's ownership to Mom so I told Randy I would be helping her, suggesting he hire someone to take my place.

Meanwhile, I gathered Dad's account books and brought them home. Mom and I spent day and night in his study around his worn desk, immersed in pages covered with his neat, handwritten figures. I drank pot after pot of Mom's coffee. She seemed to sense my exhaustion point and would sweeten our last cup with Dad's whiskey, saying this was to help us unwind.

The more I dug, the madder I got. By the end of a month, we untangled what Dad had probably discovered a hundred times faster than Mom and I ever would. The figures didn't lie. Production and profits were above normal. Dad had built Port Hetty Seafood into a profitable business, but glossed over by a shrewd Julian, glutting the profits with his big income and healthy entertainment allowance, the money that should have been there, simply wasn't. Dad had taken the reins by firing Julian, but seeing no embraceable cure for the company's ills—just like Mom declared—defeat killed him.

Already longing to turn Julian into fish bait, now came the realization that if I'd paid more attention to what was going on, Dad might still be around.

One by one, I visited the most neglected creditors. I explained the reserveless situation up front. Then, from my six years of Air Force back-pay, to each I paid a substantial sum to prove my good intentions. Next, I contacted the Veterans Administration to see if the G.I. Bill of Rights could grant me funds to nourish the business. Knowing this would take time, and that I might lose a few of the seafood and equipment suppliers in the interim, I prepared to hunt for replacements.

The employees listened silently while I revealed the company's status. They had not missed a paycheck yet, I reminded them, and promised to do my level best to see they didn't. After my announcement, several longtime workers came to the office and offered money or to go without pay for a month or two. Inspired by their loyalty, I thanked them, insisting I would like to test my theory first—that I could turn the business back to profitability—but that if I failed, they would be the first to know.

I had almost wiped out my independence, but as my first mission, I vowed to guarantee Mom's. And in a silent eulogy to Dad, I made another, more relentless pledge: With the help of the faithful and hard work, I meant to revitalize the business.

I thought about confronting Julian, considering his weighty withdrawals, but decided it was too late for that, too. Julian didn't have the money and that brought up the subject of how they would survive. I would get a second job or beg before I'd allow those kids or my sister to go hungry.

The next day, I drove to Charlotte's and discovered I was none too soon. After she admitted she hadn't seen Julian in several days, all I had to do was look around to convince myself not only was he worthless, but he left them in an emergency state. There was little food in the house, and after some badgering, Charlotte finally agreed to show me a stack of unpaid bills. Realizing her pride must take second place to their needs, she offered modest resistance when I wrote her a check.

From there on out—reminiscent of my post-college days—and with skimpy knowledge—which I found grossly out-dated—my days at the factory began at six in the morning, and never ended before that time in the evening. I jumped in, asked millions of questions along the way, spent hours studying the state's new Department of Conservation regulations—focusing on anything that might influence production—and familiarized myself with new and old equipment.

Along with digesting the modernization of the fishing industry—boats equipped with freezer tanks in their holds, fleets that owned or chartered light seaplanes to search for tuna schools—each new concept in that area forced me to look more closely at our packing and shipping business.

Innovations abounded there, too. My head spun with talk of labor unions and distributors' names. It ached from reading reports and studying mountains of charts. I read brochures touting leaps in production with the purchase of everyone's "superior" or "expanded" processing methods or equipment for perishables. Quick freezing—with the latest craze for fish sticks, meal-sized portions, and ready to cook meals, were in. Prehistoric, sun-drying techniques that used to take from ten to fourteen days, were passé. A machine, made up of a drying tunnel, an engine, a fan and an oven to keep the air dry, and taking less than thirty-six hours, replaced that method.

Stylish packaging—found to promote popularity, in turn boosting sales—and better transportation deadlines, were in. Scrap and waste contracts for fertilizer, animal food, oil and meal factories, along with import and export—all in.

It didn't take long for me to see the scales were tipped toward appearance and convenience. With that realization came concern—or recognizing the lack of—for cleanliness and freshness, so this became my panacea. Grading, cleaning and cutting for machines or hand packing, laws regulating the type of boats and gear, the net mesh size as well as their length and depth, the period of the fishing season, the number of fishing days permitted, although still observed, seemed to have fallen out of favor.

I read the Department of Conservation's annual reports and bulletins from the United Nations Food and Agricultural Organization. I watched exporters and buyers examine the catch. I learned about factory owned cold storage and freezer ships that could freeze fish at sea for sale later, allowing crews to stay out for long stretches and go great distances to look for fish.

The use of dynamite and hand grenades—especially after the World Wars—had been prohibited because the valuable fish sank to the bottom when their air bladders are destroyed, and the young fish were hurt or killed. To learn these methods were still a raging duel between the fishermen and the Seafoods Division, struck me dumb.

Contemplating our future, my goals appeared more prohibitive. Fish, their food and their habits became secondary to how fast a nylon net can be shot, that now hauling the net is worked by winches, saving crew and time, and that meeting and matching the demands of modern times was now a prerequisite.

Gone were the days of Captains with a "right nose" finding favorable fishing grounds, of antlers or tail fins nailed to the crows' nest of vessels for legendary good luck. Now they were replaced by electronic detecting instruments and the most efficiently designed fishing gear based on technical calculations. Everything I read or heard led me to believe "luck" no longer influenced the success of fishing.

What a chore for the Division of Seafoods. Entrusted with the preservation, regulation and improvement of the state's seafoods industries, they were forced to hire more help and buy more patrol boats. Law enforcement, particularly in the shrimp and oyster trade, busied itself with setting up radar for detecting and breaking up illegal night harvesting, undersized oystering, or improper culling. Once again, man posed a greater threat than nature's starfish and oyster conch predators.

A prime example, with all our progress, was pollution. Whether accidental or purposeful, this loomed as an impediment, and possible destruction, to our environment.

But on the bright side, in lieu of tax payments, oystermen

can now return shells to reefs, playing a part in reaping the benefits of their future. I read how scientists and experts from all over the world shared knowledge and trained workers in the industry, impressing upon them the importance of growth and reproduction to our resources.

Every coastal state now has marine biologists conducting long range studies aimed at the preservation of existing quality and quantity. And a surprise to me, as a veteran, I was issued a free business license.

In the evenings after supper, my mind muddled by the day's tasks, routinely I settled down with Mom and the books.

Weeks passed, but the long hours, and the mental exhaustion, almost as depleting as working for Randy, proved a cure for heartache, and at Mom's insistence, I had taken a Sunday off.

The overcast morning glazed and blackened the water, and I knew if it and my mood lasted I would never get anything done, but I continued to waste the day in my hammock. Telling myself I'd earned a break, I wrestled with the awareness my life wasn't turning out exactly the way I planned and in spite of fatigue, I knew I needed to make some changes.

For the first time in a long, long while, I thought about Rhea. We'd had quite a showdown the night before Dad died. I rushed over after her guests left and her house darkened. Drunk and willful, when she opened the door, I grabbed her and kissed her passionately only to feel her pushing, finally shoving, me away.

After an easy-going six months, our camaraderie ignited the night of her exhibit, and for two days and nights, she woke a hunger in me I thought had starved and died, more passion than I knew existed, even with the consuming love I'd had with Mandy. We loved hard and tender, quickly and slowly, but above all I'd believed we'd blazed the way for an unconditional love. Afterward, with her in New York, I'd pined like a teenager, dreamily planning her return, scribbling her name on anything that lay close at hand, gazing at her empty, dormant house and remembering the feel of her skin, her taste, her touch. I should have known it was too good to be true when several weeks turned into six, and when she announced that unscheduled trip to Paris, something poisonous happened.

But back to the night of our battle. Already a little imprudent with desire, she'd pushed me over the rim when she'd said that night was a mistake—she'd been drunk—and she was sorry.

"Don't give me that crap!" I'd barked. "Tell me you were wrong, tell me you've met someone else, but don't say…"

"All right! I was wrong!"

"I don't believe you," I whispered, sliding to my knees. I wrapped my arms around her legs and held on. "Rhea—Rhea, don't do this," I heard myself beg, and didn't care.

All she would say was our lifestyles were too conflicting, our interests too dissimilar and that I was too devouring.

Stunned, I left. I wanted to get away from the inconsistencies—no, lies—they had to be lies! streaming from her mouth. What happened to the promises of undying love? Oh, I see. That traded places with regret. Sure, I understand. No, no need to ask forgiveness for what sounded like commitment, and I laughed hysterically when she suggested we remain friends.

Suddenly, we stood in a steady, cold rain facing each other. Thunder boomed, lightening flashed and I honestly believed she'd unleashed the gods' hostility with her condemnation. With sadness in my heart, I reached out and traced a rivulet down her face and asked if she had forgotten somewhere in our not too distant history whispering, "I love you, too"? A thunderbolt charged the earth, exploded and in its illumination I searched her icy face. "Tell me the truth. Did I imagine making love to you that night? Did I imagine your words? Please, tell me, Rhea."

Rain dripped from her hair. I took her hands. They were steady; only mine trembled, and there was no way I could defend myself from her words stabbing my soul when she denied everything. This time I staggered home and began my desensitizing that lasted to the night of Dad's massive heart attack. But to this day, I still couldn't imagine what cruel circumstance could have changed her mind so easily. You don't just love a person passionately one moment and with nothing but time and space in-between, decide you don't love them anymore!

Twelve

    Near twilight, I watched a green dragonfly dart onto the porch and perch on the handrail, balancing steady and sure, eyeing me along with the whole universe in a single bulbous glance. I froze, but it left and I wanted to go, too.
    Instead, deciding to take a night off, I drove to town and stopped in Sloopy's for a beer. Thin girls swayed from side to side with guys in cowboy hats to the beat of twangy country music. I sat on a stool, sipped my beer, and soon the girls winking and giggling without any results, ignored me. Feeling lonelier than ever, I thought about Rhea, what she might be doing and paid my tab.
    There was one other stop I needed to make. I drove to the

harbor and walked down the wooden pier. The Dizzy Dame glistened in the moonlight and I nodded, thinking Randy must have found some good, deserving first mate to take my place. As I strolled closer, I realized Randy had company. The large, red-faced man shaking his fist at my brother looked familiar and when I heard Randy say coolly, "Harold, my price is firm," I recognized the man from his twin—Happy Harold's Used Cars—pasted on several billboards around town. Well, old Harold didn't look or sound too happy at the moment. On his sign, Harold held a fistful of ten dollar bills, supposedly offering the savings to gullible customers, but under the pier's floodlights he sneered viciously and sweated on this cool spring night.

Lingering in the shadows, I let their argument drift to me. Old Harold tried in vain to haggle Randy's price down. I puffed up with pride, seeing my brother shake his head repeatedly. Randy's back was to me so I couldn't hear everything he said, but looking at Harold's face, I knew Randy had come a long way since the days he would have made a mid-air lunge for the money.

Harold's dissertation on youth's lack of respect for hard-earned cash continued. I wondered how Randy kept from laughing in the man's face; the epitome of indulgence jiggled in his blubbery belly, and his splotched face dripped water like he'd just run a marathon. Reminding me of an Olympian athlete, Randy's muscles strained the seams of his tee shirt while he warped rope from elbow to palm with the grace of a practiced sailor.

Suddenly, Randy whirled and started toward me stopping just as quickly when he spied me in the shadows, surprise flowing across his youthful face. He tied off the ropes end, and as though Harold disintegrated once he'd turned his back and moved from the light, Randy tossed the coil aside and came at me with open arms. Harold stomped off the pier, Randy and

I opened a beer and two hours and a six-pack later, we left arm in arm.

Back at Mom's, I told her Randy and I healed our misunderstanding, that I'd eaten dinner with him and Diane, and that he gave me some lifesaving ideas for the business: things like who would pay their bills and who wouldn't; who would give good advice and who not to trust even if their hand rested on a Bible. After she went up to bed, I pulled the books out again to compare last years poundage to present landings, another tip from Randy. Supply didn't seem to pose a problem. Imports weren't threatening. New, stricter regulations could touch the whole industry harder, but everyone would be in the same boat. Unless some unforeseen disaster fell in my lap, within a few months I should be able to pay expenses and feed the mouths, possibly reach a notable profit margin. If I could manage that, making good my guarantee to the employees and the distributors, I could breath a sigh of relief and restore honor to Dad's lifelong undertaking.

Tonight, I made a new, poignant discovery. Ever since Dad's death, I had methodically sorted through all the files and drawers in his desk at home. This project would be completed after I cleaned out the bottom right-hand drawer, so I removed everything and found my father's diary. It looked exactly like the red and green ones my sisters used to keep, but Dad, always more subdued in character and attire, choose a conservative brown one. I sat down in the middle of the clutter and turned it over and over, amazed that the stern man I'd known harbored a clandestine side that allowed him to write down his thoughts in a journal, much less hide it away in a corner. To the outsider, no more sensible, cautious or honest businessman existed, but from working by his side in the past, I also knew no more approachable, charitable or compassionate man lived than my father. Maybe that's why he turned to this little logbook. Everyone crowded him with their problems and certainly having some of his own, this must have slaked his need. Couldn't he go to Mom? She did convey a prim air. Working closely with her since Dad's death, I found her strict, frugal and masterfully unswerving, but at times downright bullheaded.

The small, but thick leather-bound book wasn't locked; a clear certainty he believed no one suspected he'd keep such a thing! Did Dad's longing for empathy, friendship and reassurance drive him to this means? The possibility of that tugged at my heart-strings.

I thumbed through the pages, then flipped back to the last entry and saw he had written in it up to two nights before he died. Before I grasped what I had done, I had read back six months. At two in the morning, I shut the book, wiped tears from my face and sat in the dark for a long time, wishing I could tell my father what he meant to me, too.

"Someday," I told my mother, "—and this may sound strange—I'd like to see the Bridge of No Return again. Do you realize I spent more years on the other side of it than I was married to Mandy, than I spent in college, than I... Anyway, I've got this preoccupation, Mom—I don't know why—to go back."

"Did you leave something behind?"

"Maybe. But beneath those camouflage nets, behind those concrete and barbed wire bunkers or just the other side of those northern mountain ranges, thousands of American soldiers may still need someone to come look for them." I shrugged off the ugly memories. Hunting for a way back to this peaceful scene of soft lights, low conversation, a cup of coffee with an aging woman of such scrupulous beauty who loved me no matter what, in the underground caverns of my soul, I hungered for that total energy tying me to Rhea. Like Dad, I yearned for attention, tenderness and that unique sign revealed to souls and bodies thrust together by some fluke of nature—like water to blood, like faith to theology. Yet discontentment filled my life because I knew what I lacked, And it's wrong! I wanted to shout. "And there's something else I'd like to do. Dad had been researching the Kipling's—did you know that?" Maybe I'll get another chance. Maybe she'll think about it and…

"Yes," Mom replied, covering a yawn.

She was tired. These days, with no one expecting me and nowhere to go, I seemed to rummage around inside and out of my body like a hungry, wide awake, stray dog, overlooking others' needs. "I hate to admit it, but I'd never given a thought to being related to Rudyard…" Oh, Rhea! What happened? Forget it! Chances are next to none, the none very much a reality. "I mean, he was Dad's first cousin, for crying out loud!

"I remember Dad reading *Captain's Courageous* to me, telling me he had this cousin who wrote about animals who talk, fought women's suffrage and whose only son died in World War II." That's good! Now you're getting her off your mind.

"That's where you get your Roman nose, your romantic point of view and your adventuresome nature," Mom confessed. "You're the epitome of kindness and caring—to a fault. I'm afraid the Birdsong's lacked those generous qualities." Laughing, she rose and straightened the crocheted arm pieces on her chair, clasped her hands and peered all-knowing at me over glasses balancing on the end of her nose. "Patience, Kip. Everything will work out."

Mantovani's violin's finished "Charmaine" and another record dropped. The noise startled me but my heart kept right on breaking. For the last hour, I'd stared into space with one thing on my mind: Rhea.

I picked up Mom's Encyclopedia Britannia's 1954 Year Book and began reading. "In June, after long hearings, the

Atomic Energy Commission refused to renew security clearance on physicist J. Robert Oppenheimer. Dr. Oppenheimer has been in charge of developing the A-bomb and is found guilty of—not disloyalty but only of vague and wholly legal proclivities—having Communist friends and lacking enthusiasm for the H-bomb project. He has been fired as consultant..."

Marking my place, I laid the book aside and walked out onto the deck. The pleasant weather—and a sense of foreboding—rested on my chest like a fallen tree, causing me to open all the doors and windows. With every fiber of strength I possessed, I tried not to look at her house, but in the corner of my eye, I knew lights blazed and my curiosity got the best of me. My heart soared! Rhea was walking down on the beach, her bright house lighting her pathway like a beacon in the dark night. She was alone and heading my way!

She looked up. I started to wave but she dropped her head and kept walking. There's no doubt in my mind she saw me. Even though it's dark, lights from my house should make me visible. She can't hide from me. Should I go down and meet her? Trust your instincts and be patient! Independent of the truth and for sanity's sake—mine—I thought hard, trying to deduce how her mind dealt with what we'd shared, and how she'd neatly tucked it into oblivion. Such passion! Such drama! She must truly be one fine actress!

Rhea's denial had given punishment new meaning, but in those next moments I suffered ten times worse than any day in the POW camp. So while I prayed for her to keep on coming, I knew she held my salvation in her hands, and that I'd kneel at her feet, beg, take all the blame, never question anything she did or said to make love consume us again. But there was no hesitancy in her stride; she passed the house, me, and hope.

Shadows blotted out her figure, and as if sucked into oblivion, she disappeared. In agony, I shut my mind to the bolting of my pulse, lethargically moved inside, tore off my clothes and let the shower cool my fevered body. Resting my head against the slick tile, I changed the temperature, waiting now for the heat and steam to soothe my jangled nerves. Afterwards, body and soul in a battle of wits, I pulled out my kite making supplies, measured and cut sticks, paper and string and struggled to immersed my thoughts. The spine's off balance. I can wait. Measuring cloth for the tail—seven times the length of the spine. But I can't stand living next door and not even speaking!

I'd done such a good job, it took her calling my name to get my attention. When I looked up from where I sat on the floor, she stood in the open door. The wind billowed her gossamer dress into the room, flipped her hair over, almost hiding her face, and I thought I was hallucinating until, straight out of a fifty cent novel, she said, "Mike, we need to talk."

For a second, I just stared. Somehow I made it to the door, took her hand and pulled her inside. I brushed damp hair from her mouth, her cheeks and drew her to me. When I felt her warmth, I closed my eyes and held on to her trembling body, afraid to say a word for fear I'd wake up and she'd be gone again. It's true! Feeling her in my arms, everything I'd been afraid to remember rushed back, and I knew it all did happen. Sweetly familiar, her nearness invoked such bedlam to my insides there was no way I could deny the foggy, crazy, make-believe dream I'd pretended, never happened.

Tipping her face up to mine, I swept her wet cheeks with kisses, touched her eyelids with my lips and tasted the tears on her lashes. I found her mouth and she slipped her arms around my neck. I gathered her closer and when she parted her lips,

I spun skyward, soared through the clouds and into space with joy. The flowery scent of her, the heady urging of her warm mouth, her fingers raking through my hair, her body toiling against mine, freed me from reason.

Collecting her in my arms, I lay her on the sofa and pushed the ruffles from her shoulders. Cupping both breasts in my hands, I kissed first one nipple then the other and she moaned. Nuzzling the valley between those noble peaks, I felt her hips lift to meet mine when I moved over her, and I came alive.

Suddenly, her palms shoved against my shoulders and she cried, "Oh, God, no! Mike, no! NO!"

Straddling her legs, I sat back on my haunches, watching wide-eyed while she wrestled with her blouse, clutching it about her neck. I rolled my head back, face to the ceiling and clapped my hands to my ears, gulping air, and waited. What ravishing new torture came next? Of all idiotic tricks, a line from a poem seared through my head: "Woman! The gate of hell!" and I laughed out loud.

Moments before writhed a burning jewel beneath me, now there lay a statue, straight from one of her paintings with only the faintest twitch and the shallow rise and fall of her bosom to vouch that she lived and breathed.

Shifting my weight, I set my right foot on the floor, raised my body, and slithered away, kneeling beside her. I took her hand in mine, pressed it to my lips, and cried like a baby. "Rhea, I can't bear this. I love you too much not to obey your wishes. Just then, if I'd thought you didn't really want me to stop, I wouldn't have. But the conviction in your voice—only a demented man—which you'll never know how close you've driven me to—could go through with an act so plainly distasteful to you.

"You're sucking the life from me—and I don't much care—but if I live to be the next Methuselah—but right now I feel three parts dead—I'll never understand what you want of me."

All this time, she hadn't moved. Her fingers fidgeted with the cloth at her throat and her unseeing eyes blinked in cadence.

It took the last of my strength to keep from shaking her, or slapping her, so certain I'd become that she'd sunk into a trance. "Rhea—" No response. I sighed heavily, shoved my weight upward and walked to the door. My knees quaked. Outside, I dropped into a canvas chair and stared out to sea.

When she stood before me, squatted and lay her hands on my knees, our eyes locked, and I had no sense of time passing. There was no fluttering in my heart, no constriction in my groin—we'd switched places. Before me, the woman I loved prepared to make the last incision and remove my heart, and I wondered if she would be surprised to see no blood. Somehow, sometime, her carnal leeches had already done their job on my body and soul. An empty, exhausted, bewildered shell sat watching her. She alone held the power to pump breath into this framework, or as an alternative, if she choose, to squash the remains.

"This will be as difficult for you to understand as it was for me. Along the way, I concluded you should have some voice, although I must add your choices are limited.

"I'm pregnant, Mike. It is your child. Lowell and I—I had not let him touch me in the months leading up to our—to our lovemaking, so I'm sure about its origin. I knew this would be a question in your mind."

I reached out for her, but she held up her palm, then touched her fingertips to my lips.

"Please, hear me out. I did not go to Paris. When my suspicions were confirmed, I took an apartment in New York because I needed time to think. I know you love me, and bitch that you'll believe me to be, I've made a selfish, but I feel, fair decision. At first, without your ever knowing, I'd decided to have an abortion. So you see, regardless of what you presume, I do have some compassion.

"There's one other thing I think you should know. I let you make love to me because I knew it might be my only chance. From a very reliable source, your mother, I learned right before I left that Mandy intends to win you back. She's divorcing her husband, she and her baby are living at her parents, here in town, and before long, you'll find yourself in the middle of a nasty divorce. Trey, I believe is his name, is going to fight.

"Your mother also told me what a great love you and Mandy had, and Mike, I would never stand in the way of you having that happiness again. You deserve it.

"Now, what I propose is to have your baby, if you wish." She rose, smoothed her hands against her stomach and revealed a small mound. "As you can see, it's too late to do otherwise. Once the baby is born, I will put it up for adoption if you and Mandy don't want it, and I'll certainly understand if she's not agreeable."

"I want our baby!"

"I felt sure you would." A new flood of tears poured from her eyes. "Mike, no matter what you think of me, please believe me when I say, I do love you." She wiped her face with both hands.

"Oh, Rhea…"

"Wait! I do, Mike, but what I didn't gamble on was the pregnancy. The big problem is my career. Tell me how a woman who paints day and night and travels all over the world can have a baby?"

"Rhea—Just marry me, have our child, and I'll hire someone to care for the baby until I get home. You won't have to lift a finger unless it holds a paint brush. I'll do whatever it takes. At least think about it! I love you, Rhea. I'm not in love with Mandy anymore. I can't go back to her, Rhea! Don't you understand? What we have, especially now, is so much more important, so much more valuable…"

"I need to go, Mike. You talk to Mandy. You think, and let me think. We'll talk in a week or two."

Thirteen

If only I'd thought about the consequences when I rushed Mike into an affair! It's not enough that he's drowning in nightmares and enduring sinister harassments! No! Now I've caused him more problems by letting myself become pregnant, deciding to keep the baby and offering it to him and Mandy! Of course she won't want it! Why didn't I take matters into my own hands while there was still time? What an effrontery, but now I have no alternative. The truth of the matter is I didn't want to harm the fruit of our love, so if there's a possibility of Mandy and Mike getting back together—and I must encourage their reconciliation—I pray they'll take our child. I may be expecting the absurd, but Mike's vow proved that fear baseless.

Over the last week, we've hardly seen one another. I can only imagine what's going on in his head, and I'm not sure I've done the fair thing after all. One thing I have learned. Love clouds your judgment. About the time you believe you've taken the right course and said the right words, the world tumbles in on you like the proverbial precarious house of cards. My whole being screams out to go to him, but in the past I've been self-centered and this time I want to do what's best for this man who means the world to me. There! You've said it!

It's getting late. The air's suddenly still; even the waves are resting. A candle moth breaks into my silence when it flutters under the lamp shade, breaking up the light with its battling shadows. I watched while the delicate insect threw itself time and again toward the deadly heat and wondered what it was thinking. Didn't it have enough brains to figure out it caused itself this pain? Don't we? Does God shake his head in wonder when we senselessly slam ourselves against what is hurtful? Is that why I sat through the night deciding that today I'll give in to my voracious need to see him, go over and invite him to dinner. It's a start!

I don't know what I expected, but when I neared his house, I saw him lolling in the hammock beneath an unusually cruel spring sun. His eyes were dull and heavy-lidded. I'd never seen him smoke before and realized what he held tightly between two fingers was no ordinary cigarette. Five or six beer cans lay on the ground around him, and he held another. He lifted a hand in greeting. Just as quickly he let it drop and dangle over the edge of the canvas sling. As I drew nearer I smelled the smoke's sweet mustiness.

As though—which will it be, God or Satan?—drove me here, as though the past months are yet to be or have never been, telling myself it's time to span the abyss between us, if it's not too late, I invited him to dinner. He sucked on the stub, smoke wound around his fingers and curled out his mouth when he thanked me, saying he had plans.

"Right now?"

"Huh?"

"I'm talking about right now, Mike!" The inclination to get some food into his stomach became urgent. "Evidently your plans are not immediate. I'll toss a big salad and you can open the wine."

He pitched forward. I expected him to fall on his face, but he sat up, pushed from the hammock and stood swaying before me. He held the cigarette butt out to me. I shook my head, brushed damp hair from my forehead, and he flipped it off into the sand. A voice inside me said, Help him! but another said, Run!

"How's our muffin?" he asked, touching my belly lightly.

"Growing."

He nodded. His eyes narrowed, and he scanned my face critically. "Are you getting enough exercise? Are you eating right?"

"Yes." I stepped backward, ready to flee.

A group of terns flew by and squawked angrily. Laughing, he said, "Silly birds," but I wondered if something had frightened them. Should I be wary too? He took a wobbly step toward me. He'd never hurt me, but he was groggy and I wondered how long he'd been mistreating himself, if he'd seen Mandy, or if... "Can I bring something?"

His eyes burned into mine like fire against ice. In one glance I saw passion, hurt and doubt and tried not to throw myself into his arms when he smiled crookedly and touched my cheek with one finger. I wanted to ask, What happened today? but answered, "Yourself." I wheeled and headed for the dune that separated our houses, hoping he'd be able to make it on his own.

"Yourself what?"

"Bring yourself, that's what!"

"That's a poor excuse for a meal. Salad and wine?"

"Shut up and come on. I'll fix some hot bread or something. Have you ever left hungry from one of my meals?" I glanced over my shoulder. He hadn't made a move to follow.

"Nope."

"Well, then—"

"I'm a mess," he yelled. "I'll be over after I shave."

"I'm not offended by your stubble. Rather striking as long as you don't try to kiss me." Maybe I shouldn't joke with him in this state. He'll probably take it as a dare and I'll be in deep distress because of my own weakening nerve.

"Nope, tried that. Didn't work. I'm probably smelly as today's catch, too." Regardless of the lame excuses rolling from his mouth, I could tell without looking around he was following now by the way his words jerked and halted. When I reached my steps, I heard a thud. Positive he'd fallen, I thought Who needs this! but knew that was the devil's manipulating words inside me. I did need him! I longed to hold him and console him, but that's what got us into this mess! But what if we're destined to be together? What if I'm driving him away only to make both our lives miserable? If we weren't intended to be together why do we keep trying? "I know, you can pay penance by washing up afterwards."

"Me?"

"The dishes!"

"Oh, in that case, I think I'll take a rain check…"

At that moment, Delilah found us. Full of energy and trying to decide who'd be most likely to play, she skid in the sand at my feet, whirled and raced to Mike, back to me and I almost lost my balance when she brushed my legs. "Delly! Enough!" Mike shouted, running up and grabbing the ungainly dog. "You mind your manners," he scolded. "Our buddy's in a delicate condition, and we must take care of her!" Like a reproached child, the animal's soft brown eyes surveyed me, she hung her head and plopped down beside the steps. By this time, I'd reached the porch. I heard Mike laughing and looked back. He lay on his back, Delilah straddling his chest and her long wet tongue washed his face. "Help! I'm being attacked by a vicious beast! Help!"

Determined to ignore his ploy, I shoved the sliding glass door aside, stamped sand from my feet and marched into the kitchen. Oddly enough, I felt invigorated and wanted to frolic up and down the beach with Mike and Delilah, but mingled with this, whether over his self-destructive demeanor or his light-heartedness—I wasn't sure—an exasperated part of me wanted to yell at the top of my lungs for him to act like an adult! Hormonal instability? Whatever, I longed to tell him our baby moved, slept, laughed and cried. I yearned for him to hold me when I laughed and cried, to tell me he loved me, the baby and make brave plans for our future, and yet I'm suddenly mad as hell, but as soon as I looked at him it withered, and I knew there's no need to waste time on petty emotions.

He stood in the doorway brushing sand off his legs and grinning a villainous little boy grin full of anticipation, full of courage. Just as quickly, a downcast expression new to me crossed his face, and I saw anxiety flicker sadly in his eyes.

"Are you in a hurry?"

I looked down. I'd ripped the lettuce and tossed it into the wooden bowl, now I glared at him while I viciously hacked a tomato. "You're the one with other plans. I'm just trying to be accommodating."

"You're mad."

Waving the blade of the knife, I whirled to face him. "Yes, I guess I am." He cringed, and I almost laughed thinking I saw fear in his eyes, and immediately hated myself for enjoying his soberness. "Oh, Mike! I'm trying to understand… Trying to make sense out of our lives... Trying to do what is best, but I'm warning you, if you keep this trend up, I'll change my mind about letting you have the baby. I'm not sure you're fit to raise a child."

"No! Don't say that!" He rose. His chair fell backwards, but he ignored it. He placed both hands on the counter, and when I looked up, I could tell he was almost in tears. I stopped slicing and listened. "I'll never drink another beer. I'll do whatever you say, but I know one thing, Rhea, I can't stay here. Living next door... It won't work. It hurts too much. I'm moving in with Mom. I can't see you... know you're so close... The only reason I did that stuff today... Well, let's just say I'd made a monumental decision I'm not particularly happy about, but I'll take good care of our child and..."

A thunderous noise drowned out his words, split the night like drums from Heaven being pounded; even the wind whipped up evilly. I looked out the kitchen window and saw three white lights probing the twilight's dusky blue. Mike moved beside me, looked out and said, "Looks like I've got company." He swatted the light switch, plunging us into inkiness, blinding me, but I knew he moved away.

I clutched at space. "No, don't go out there!" I heard the door creak. Motors revved loudly, their noised filling the inside of my head. Delilah barked. "Mike!" I whispered. "Don't leave me..." but I knew he'd gone. I clamped my hands over my ears and called after him again not to leave me, but the din blanketed my words.

"Get down, Rhea, and stay here!"

I dropped to the floor, heard a muffled thud, then another. Delilah barked non-stop now, and I thought I heard Mike calling her. A boom shook the floor beneath my feet; the windows rattled. Silence. Popping and roaring rent the air. An orange glow flickered around the room. I eased to the end of the cabinets, raised up and pulled the curtain aside. Mike's house sat like a huge box engulfed in flames. I choked back a scream. Where was he? He hadn't had time to reach his house, but all I could hear was the trumpet of machines mingled with the roar of flames.

My heart raced, thumping in unison with the motors. The baby elbowed me hard, and I grunted. A different cracking—clearer and nearer—hurt my ears. Delilah yelped. I heard Mike shout and footsteps pounding up my outside stairs. "Oh, Mike! Come inside. Don't go out there again!" I cried, rushing toward the porch.

But then, above the loud whir and whine of motors, I heard Mike yell, "This is private property! I've called the police," and it struck me that's what I should do. I ran to the phone and dialed frantically. I heard Mike growl, "You bastards! What have you done…" Someone, not Mike, laughed crudely and cursed. Answer, damnit, answer! A monotone voice slurred out some police station and I jabbered my story. They promised to send someone right away and I heard more cracking. "I think they're shooting at us," I snapped over the phone. They told me to stay down, they'd be here soon.

I had to know if Mike was all right. I slithered out the door. Hugging the rough exterior, I peeked around the side of the house. Coming from his house, Mike staggered with the weight of something big in his arms. It's Delilah!

All at once, someone grabbed my hair, yanking my head back. My hands clawed the air, grasping for anything. A hand grabbed one of my arms and cruelly twisted it behind my back, pitching me to my knees. I screamed. My hair was released, and a hand, reeking of gas, locked over my mouth. I tried to bite the skin, desperately clawing the air with my free hand as I was dragged down the steps. Finally, I found my attacker's head, what felt like a ski mask and tugged. Then I grabbed a handful of hair. My assailant howled.

"Julian! Julian, let her go." We were halfway down the

steps. I was shoved against the rail and felt... Julian! Mike called the man holding me Julian! I tried to look around, but felt something cold press against my temple and froze. I shifted my eyes toward Mike. He'd dropped Delilah and ran toward us. "I'll do whatever you say. Just don't harm her, Julian. Please."

Julian squatted behind me, squeezing against my body. I could feel his hot, rapid breath on my neck, and violent trembling. He's scared! Julian's the one trembling! "Well, you've done it now, toots," Julian snarled in my ear. "Stay where you are!" he yelled at Mike. "I've got a gun pointed at your girlfriend's head, Mike, and I'll kill you both if I have too!"

"For God's sake! She hasn't done anything to you! Let her go! We'll talk this over!"

"Sometimes you're not very bright, Mikey, old buddy. I can't let her go. I can't let either of you go now."

"Sure you can. Is it the money? Don't worry. That's water over the dam." Calmly, Mike chattered, diverting Julian, and hope returned when I felt his grip loosen. "I'll even forget all this. Let her go, and I'll forget the letters, the dead animals... You did all that, didn't you?"

"No law says I can't send letters. Dead animals don't hurt anyone."

"Laws say you can't do this, Julian. You're burning my house. That's arson. But I'm willing to call it even if you let her go. I'll forget you've killed my dog, too. She wouldn't have hurt you or your partners, just got in your way, huh? So before you go too far and hurt someone, put the gun down, and let's talk."

"The damn dog attacked me! Besides, it's not that simple, brother-in-law! Too bad, too. I know she's carrying your bastard!"

Our baby! He called our baby a bastard! Howling,

omnipotent anger soared through my body, and like Wonder Woman bursting from a comic book's pages, miraculously I rose upright, freed my arms and shoved Julian. The gun exploded. Julian toppled, but grabbed my blouse, and we tumbled down the planks.

My head hit something solid. Pain burned behind my eyes, but Mike was holding me, whispering to me. A neanderthal roar dove at us, and Julian, with blood running down the side of his face, slugged Mike's head with the gun. Mike rolled, shook his head and struggled to his hands and knees. Julian pointed the gun at his head, and I lunged for Julian's feet. The gun went off. From the corner of my eye, I saw Mike crumple and I lost all mercy. I leaped for the gun, locked my hands over Julian's and held fast. We fell back, thrashed on the sand, and suddenly, Charlotte screamed, "Julian! Stop!" He did, and I looked up.

Glowing in the firelight, Charlotte, her face twisted by horror, outrage, and glistening with tears, stood a few feet away. "How could you!" she screamed.

I'd scrambled away toward Mike, but Julian snatched me back, clamped an arm across my shoulders and jammed the gun under my chin. He shouted for Charlotte to leave. She whimpered, "I can't believe you've done this," and slowly walked toward us.

From behind, Mike growled. Julian started, and Mike flew by, landing on top of him. The gun went off again. Charlotte gasped. I heard her begging Julian not to hurt us, begging Mike to forgive her, and her voice grew faint. Julian flung Mike aside and crawled to Charlotte's body. I groped for Mike, found him and kneeling beside him, gathered him in my arms.

All at once, it grew quiet. Then, harsh sounds shattered the brief, unexpected harmony, and like prehistoric monsters the forgotten cyclists' headlights reared skyward, shiny metal gleamed and the bikers roared away. Except for the screeching blaze, darkness spread around the four of us huddled on the sand.

Then a new noise filled my ears. In the distance, the roar of the departing motors droned, but—Thank God! Sirens!—drew closer.

Nothing moved but the pulsating flames casting grotesque shadows across the sand and our cluster of bodies. I sobbed. For the first time, I saw Delilah. Her inert, wet body lay a few feet from Mike.

Smoke, and a gaseous stench filled the air. When I glanced at Mike's house, it looked like the sun, walking on stilts, had joined us, with orange tongues licking up its sides. It groaned like a dying monster, and caved in on itself.

"Oh, God!" Julian whimpered. I'd forgotten him, and I saw him kneeling beside Charlotte, moaning, "Oh, God," over and over.

"Don't hurt him anymore, Julian. Please…" Charlotte whimpered. "Mike, I'm sorry. …so sorry."

"Are you okay, Rhea?" I gasped. Mike reached up and touched my chin. I nodded. "I love you, Rhea. God knows I love you with all my heart. I…" He coughed.

"Damnit, don't you die, Mike! I'll never forgive you if you die on me, do you hear? I'll never speak to you again. I'll never let you see our child. Mike, please, stay with me! I love you! I've always loved you. Forgive me, Mike! I've been cruel, but I do love you so!"

He smiled. I sensed someone beside me, and I looked around. Two men were squatting by us, coaxing me to let Mike go. I told them to leave him alone. They promised me they were here to help him, and for the first time, I noticed people surrounded us, lights flashed over the beach, over our forlorn little group, over the houses, the water, and walking alongside, I let them take him. Another man lifted Charlotte and a policemen shoved Julian toward his patrol car.

Someone said, "Come with us, lady, we need to go."

"Just a minute, please." An officer leaned close to Mike's face. "Can you tell us who did the shooting, mister?"

"No. I don't know who they were."

"Mike!"

"I didn't recognize anyone."

They lifted Mike into an ambulance. I climbed in and sat beside him. He mumbled something. I put my ear to his mouth, nodded my head and gently kissed his lips to let him know it was true. He tried to get up, couldn't and fell back.

"Lie still, mister. You're gonna be okay."

Sluggishly, he winked at me and closed his eyes.

Fourteen

When I was a little boy, I knew I'd grow up and go to war, and I did, but it lasted longer than I expected. Back home waited a beautiful wife, a loving family, and more than likely, my old job in my father's seafood business.

After almost six years of fighting to stay alive, certain everyone back home, including the military and the politicians, had given up hope, my prayers were answered in a POW swap, and like Mandy, I got a second chance.

I was afraid when I got back everything would have changed, and with the exception of my wife—and in all honesty, Mandy did the best she could—and my grandparents—who just wore out—the rest of the family waited, but nothing else did. What I valued and clung to in respect to the world, people, and principles now seemed contrary, some good, some bad.

In my nightmares, I still worked frantically to free the cage door, to dig another tunnel, to scale a wall, or to walk off, unnoticed. Sometimes, I hear the screams of the family who died because they helped me, the screams of my buddies, and my own, but ever since I met Rhea, the horrors have tapered off.

In spite of our first exasperating meeting—the night she came knocking on my door borrowing sugar, and I upset everything within my crutches range—Rhea became my friend, my purpose in life, and later, my lover. Briefly.

Afterwards, when I told her how bad I'd wanted her to stay, she laughed and said I'd scared her by staring at her hungrily for ages. She said she knew right then something had gone wrong in my life.

I remember every detail, enjoy thinking about her long brown hair pulled up on her head, sparkly stones in her hair, and me, wondering how I could get this pretty, nosey neighbor to come back. During one of our more talkative interludes that fabulous couple of days before she left for New York, she said when I finally smiled that first day, shivers ran up her spine. I asked her to show me, and we got all caught up in lovemaking again. If I get a chance, I need to let her finish telling her side of the story.

But before we became emotionally involved and life got complicated, Rhea gave me the Dream Catcher—an Indian talisman to filter out nightmares. And the more she learned about my other problems—the threatening letters, the grisly parade of dead animals and the vandalizing—the more she tried to help. Possibly my savior, Rhea even attempted to help wipe out my more bothersome memories, and in fact, they did become less significant the more time I spent with her.

So what's the problem? The problem turned out to be me; I fell in love with her. It took realizing I'd been studying her routine—which only served to confirm several suspicions: one, she traveled a lot; another, she followed no routine; finally, at times she's brutally blunt—for me to accept this fact.

Then, quite suddenly, for two days and nights, we loved, the type of love you only read about in poetry or novels, but to date, with no "happily ever after" finale—but there's always hope! To really thicken the plot, Rhea discovered she was pregnant. She panicked, but thank goodness, she told me, and perturbed as she was—a child fit nowhere in her plans—she agreed to have our baby. I only loved her more for this sacrifice.

And then tonight, following her to her house, I noticed the men on motorcycles lined up at the pavement's edge, staring blankly at the sea, but woozy from self-destructing again, I paid little attention. It was my brother-in-law, Julian, who turned out to be the enemy. In a fit of dread and hostility, he reached his breaking point, and attacked the woman I loved. This should have been his problem, but I fought him, and his weapon was more powerful.

So now, as I feel my blood drain from my body, I'm on fire to live, and once more, I'll bite and claw my way back because, if I'm not mistaken, just before they put me in the ambulance, Rhea said she loved me! I've prayed to hear those words, and thank God for Julian's poor aim.

Julian—the son-of-a-bitch—shot my dog, but she was still breathing, and maybe they can patch us both up. He also set my house on fire, but at least I'm not headed back to my prison cell like I imagined at one point, and Rhea's safe. Rhea! You are safe, aren't you? Good!

So I've taken a slug or two—I think I heard someone say I had one in my side and one in my knee. That was Julian's bullets, not sand, scattering the ground all around us. And the stinging in my face, arms and legs turned out to be the losing consciousness bit, nothing to do with my hazy thoughts of Chinese catching up with me again. Where's the gun? Gotta make Julian let Rhea go! I lurched upward, driving for Julian's swimming face.

Hands press me back. "Easy, buddy. Just lie still."

With the noise of an air-raid alert going off around us—I guess we're on the way to a hospital—silly chronological facts flood my head. What a gluttonous student I'd been when I returned, and for a while I wondered if the world had gone crazy during the time I'd been fighting for it. Right then, in the middle of chaos, I worried about dictators who declared, "We'll bury you!" What kind of rude humanity would tag a presidential candidate "egghead?" What statement were college students making by wearing "Apache" haircuts?

Rhea hugged me, and it hurt, but it was heaven! Some guy sitting with us keeps saying I'm doing fine, but I'm having trouble focusing, fading in and out of the present. My mind's clear. At least I thought it was until I realized... What the hell! Have I died or are the nightmares back? Rhea's trying to get me into a grinning—My, what huge chrome teeth you have!—low-slung car that's hovering several feet above the ground, saying we're late and must hurry if we want to see James Dean's movie. I tried to make her understand that we're in danger. She laughed and pointed to my chest. Now I know I'm hallucinating! I'm wearing a Hawaiian shirt. She says I look good in bright green, hibiscus red and daffodil yellow. God, I can't tell her Tess gave me that shirt.

But there's always the paintings. Through them she's told me what's important. The pregnancy has scared her, but no matter. I understand.

Now what's Shallie doing here? She wants to know how many fish a pelican can hold in that big beak. Do you know, Rhea? Now it's why do men shave? And have I ever seen a horseshoe crab? And where do sea gulls go when it rains? That kid!

I'm tired, and it's a damned bumpy ride!

My God! Julian's got Rhea! No, that's not Julian. And Rhea's holding my hand, but behind her a giant, silver robot, straight from the set of *The Day The Earth Stood Still*, scooped me up and I got hysterical; laughed so hard my sides hurt. The behemoth carried me to my cell, dropped me on the floor... Letters, letters, all over the place! and I'm rolling in fits of lunacy laughing. Is that what she means when she says sometimes she sees a touch of madness in my eyes?

Another shot! This time my arm. "Huh? Oh, okay." A pretty lady said it's to take the pain away. Friendly fire! Ha! Too many faces. Too many voices. "Rhea! Stay with me!"

"You cut your hair!" Rhea said, frowning. She stood in her tight white dress, spewing her sweet beliefs, probably thinking her religious talk about the source of my nightmares made me nervous while unusual music winged in the background through her house. I asked if her guests were unusual. She didn't laugh. "That's 'Wheem-away.' You know, 'The Lion Sleeps Tonight'?" she said dramatically. I guess I should have felt stupid, but I shook my head and stifled a chuckle, visualizing her standard crowd of properly attired monkeys chanting, "Wheem-away! Wheem-away!"

Dreams. Just Dreams.

No wonder the vets were lured into the Beat Generation's mysticism! Prosperity, honor, and reason seems to have evaporated like water on the Sahara. Jazz and bebop slang? Sounds foreign to my ears, but God knows I'm trying to catch up, and I'm having a helluva a time getting folks to leave my legs alone.

Why won't she believe me? "I told you, it's so hot now, but I really did it for you! I thought you didn't like..."

"What about your hair, Mike? Don't you remember? I like it long. Everything will be okay. Just rest."

"What's Charlotte doing here! She's never come here before. Charlotte, the rifle's yours. Please, somebody! Is she okay? Is it the house? I don't want the house. Why didn't you tell Julian that, Char?"

"Who shot you, Mister?"

"I don't know."

Blackness, and Rhea's asking why I acted the way I did the night of her exhibit. "You scared the hell out of me! We'd been friends so long, I never dreamed you'd do something like that! The moon made a walkway to the shore, your face, arms, and dress glowed, and you…"

"Yes, yes, I know. I loved you at that precise moment."

"You ran from me! You looked at me like you hated me!" Why do I see Happy Harold's face on that billboard? But I'm proud of Randy for not taking any crap off that smart-alecky Harold.

"Never! How could you think…"

"Okay. It doesn't matter now. Hey, take it easy! Yeah, it hurts but not as bad as I expected."

"Please lie still, buddy."

Sure would like everyone to get quiet. I've got something important to say to Rhea. "Rhea, listen to me! I need to talk to you about our baby. I told Mandy I'm in love with you. I didn't say anything about the baby; that's our business. It's up to you, Rhea. If you feel the same, when the baby comes, I'll take him and leave."

Oh, Dad! Black, white and red fireworks are going off behind my eyelids. It hurts! It's open season on my heart and I'm tired, so tired. My ears feel full like I'm under water. Wait, Dad! Do you know why Captains grow beards? Good luck! Yes, I know I need to study the shrimp and oyster harvest graphs. Should we get into that? Yes, I know the competition's tough. We've got until late July to get ready, but even like we are, we need to replace those conveyor belts that move fish into the ship's holds faster and... What? I don't understand. Go back? Okay. Whatever you say, anyway I think Rhea's on my side now, and wouldn't she make a dazzling Queen of the Shrimp Fleet? There's lots of new stuff I can learn about preserving, storing and transporting seafood. "Where are you, Rhea? You're all I want..."

"Let's go now."

Not talking to me. "Marry me, Rhea. I'll hire someone to care for our baby until I get home." Lights, running down a hall. I can feel her eyes. I've told her how I feel, what I want, the rest is up to her.

She's curled up in a chair by me and I think I'm gonna explode with happiness. The craziest notion popped into my head, and I'm back in Rhea's kitchen, and friendly Rebecca's wrapping her tentacle-like arms around me, looking like an aging Marilyn Monroe replica: red lips, painted on dress, her words about me being Rhea's best kept secret, getting more than borderline lewd by the instant, and afterwards, Rhea saying she's harmless. Yeah, about as harmless as Heartbreak Ridge back in Korea!

But Rhea. When she opened the door and I saw the cute little wrinkle between those black, black eyebrows, all I wanted to do was make her happy. She wore a white jewel of a dress exposing one shoulder and I suddenly fantasized her as my modern-day Jane. Swinging from an imaginary vine, I wanted to grab her around the waist, spirit us to a mossy bank by a thundering waterfall where we could give lightening a new name. Instead, I told her she looked good. She thanked me, and I entered the dark recesses under her sink and bumped my head.

"Rhea?" I need to tell her the dreams she vowed to get rid

of one way or the other... I think we've hit on the cure. I've got all this energy... I reached out, took her hand and kissed her fingers. Can it be possible? "Rhea, you smell so good."

She jumped straight up. "Mike! Oh, Mike. Thank God!" She's bawling. The sun spills like gold washing her cheeks. Light and its sport kept me alive for years; she's worth a lifetime. "Don't cry. You're not leaving again, are you? Late last night, I wanted to come to you, but..." Okay, Kipling, you're not still afraid she'll get inside your head. Seal it up tight now, and you'll go home alone. "I wanted you to listen to "Moonglow" with me. You smell so good."

"I can't leave!" she sobbed. "You don't take care of yourself when I'm gone."

"And there's something else we need to talk about... What day is it?"

"It's Tuesday."

"What is that perfume you're wearing? That's not White Shoulders, is it? Are we're gonna be okay? Rhea! I just remembered..."

"It doesn't matter. You're alive and you're going to live to be one hundred. I'll see to it!"

"Does that mean what I think it means?"

"Yes."

"'Alas! The love of a woman! It is known to be a lovely and a fearful thing!' Now listen, there's a bottle of champagne in the fridge..."

"Who said that?"

"I did."

"Really!"

"I can't lie to you. Lord Byron said it first. Remember the champagne? I've just realized it works like an aphrodisiac on you. When I get home... That's right! I don't have a home!"

"You're not listening. You're stubborn, Kipling. You're with me."

"Great! Now, for chrissake, Rhea, listen to me! Yes, I do want you to kiss me, but then will you please go out and get another bottle of champagne?" She laughed. "Aren't you thirsty?" That's nice. She's kissing me, ever so softly. Ummm. Never mind.

There are nice sounds and offensive sounds. The tumbling, rushing sound of waves washing ashore, the high-pitched screech of the sea gulls, children's laughter gurgling up little throats from little souls that know no pretense; these are nice sounds. Rhea's parties have the most offensive sounds. Nothing's worse than the dull drone of dull people talking about dull subjects: themselves. But that's okay, if she's with me.

Happy Harold's back. He's gonna save us all with his handfuls of ten dollar bills, but Rhea's holding my hand, and I know now I'll be fine. I just need to rest a little longer. Then it's Rhea, me and our baby!